SARAH M. ANDERSON WRITING AS

MAGGIE CHASE

HIS TOPAZ

Acknowledgements

I could not have written this book without the generous help of the following people: Melissa Jolly for everything she does, Shae O'Conner and Laura K. Curtis for their support, Tasha Harrison and Mary Dieterich for editing, and Alexandra Haughton for designing the cover.

Dedication

To my husband

Chapter One

1866

She had made a terrible mistake.

Millie Townsend stood at the edge of the saloon in the Jeweled Ladies brothel and tried to be invisible. She had trained for almost three months to be one of the highly paid ladies of the night here and hadn't once suffered this attack of nerves.

But then again, she hadn't actually had a paying gentleman caller in those three months. Just evenings of lessons and practice with Sterling. Which hadn't been evenings filled with romance, but they hadn't left her feeling this...hollow.

Although she knew she couldn't possibly move any further back into the corner behind the bar, she tried. No one had paid for her time last night and she had been ridiculously relieved.

Somehow, she didn't think she would get so lucky a second time.

Besides, she'd chosen to do this. She wasn't a blushing virgin anymore. She was a widow at the age of twenty-one and had no other prospects. Her husband's family had pretended to care about her until it'd become clear that a week and a half of marriage hadn't resulted in a child and then Millie had been

1

unceremoniously shown the door. And she couldn't go back to Boston, where George was no doubt at this very moment trying to locate her.

She had a place to live here and a way of earning enough money to keep her safe from her half-brother. But more than that, she had anonymity.

For Millie Townsend was not hiding in a corner behind the bar in the saloon. Instead, it was Miss Topaz Gold who did so.

She surveyed the saloon, her heart beating wildly as she struggled to keep the panic at bay. The other Jewels—her new friends—were all enticing the gentleman callers, as the Mistress of the Jeweled Ladies insisted on calling the customers. Emerald all but floated into the room on the arm of the mayor, Raymond Dupree. Opal wasn't even fully dressed, for heaven's sake. Her buttons had come undone and her bodice gaped at the chest and, of course, she had hiked up her skirts to show off her garters.

Millie looked down at her gown. It was a tasteful gold—although the bodice was cut quite low and the sleeves were more of a wish than a piece of fabric. Her ankles were covered, at least.

This was the sort of gown that George would never have allowed her to buy in Boston. Of course, George had spent money on his clothes, his horses—his mistresses—while Millie had reddened her hands caring for their father and scrubbing floors in the family home.

After three months in Brimstone, Texas, her hands were once again smooth and soft. She should be excited that her new position as a Jewel afforded her the finer things in life.

If only she didn't have to spread her legs to earn them.

At least there was music tonight. Pearl often played in the parlor, but tonight she was on the small stage at the end of the saloon, banging out a jaunty tune that had many of the gentlemen callers singing along at the top of their lungs while they drank expensive spirits and gambled away their money.

Maybe she would get lucky again and no one would notice her. After all, who would look back into the shadows when Opal joined Pearl upon the stage and began to sway as the bodice of her gown crept lower and lower? Good heavens, the girl was going to disrobe on stage.

"You can't hide back here forever, you know," said Sterling Silver. In addition to training the girls under the careful direction of Mistress, he also tended the bar. He was the only one who seemed to notice her.

"I'm not hiding," she said, even though they both knew it was a lie.

"Sure you're not, honey." He wasn't looking at her, but at the glass he was drying. "Everyone works here—you know that, right?"

As he spoke, a gentleman caller bellied up to the bar and Sterling drifted away from Millie. Sterling ducked his head close to the gentleman, and the gentleman whispered in his ear.

Even Sterling worked at the Jeweled Ladies. Millie suspected that Sterling didn't just train the ladies or work the bar, though—not as the gentleman touched Sterling's chin.

The only one here who didn't work was Millie.

3

She needed to take a step forward. She had chosen this life. She had been kept in near poverty by her half-brother. She had escaped to be a mail-order bride on the assumption that marriage to a complete stranger in a hostile land was better than living under George's thumb for the rest of her life.

She had been widowed in a matter of days.

By God, she was tired of having everything taken away from her. Her parents, her husband—not that she loved him, because she hadn't. But he had been her future. Stability—a home, the promise of the children. That was gone, too.

She was tired of waiting for other people to solve her problems. That was why she was here. She was going to do her time on her back and make enough money so she would never again be subject to the cruelties of fate.

That was the plan, anyway. It hadn't worked out like that just yet.

She wasn't a shy virgin. She had married Logan Townsend within an hour of meeting him at the train depot in Henderson, Texas, and he had exercised his husbandly rights that very night and every day of their marriage on his ranch, located ten miles west of town. She'd had all kinds of sex with Sterling, including things she'd never dreamed possible.

So selecting a gentleman caller and taking him to her bed shouldn't be a big deal. She'd already spread her legs for a complete stranger before. She knew exactly what was going to happen.

She did not take another step into the light. Instead, she shrank back even further.

Just then, Mistress stepped through the door in

the saloon. As always, the madam of this brothel was dressed as if she were going to court and making her bow before a foreign king. Shimmering peach silk draped over her body and the jewels at her ears, neck and throat glimmered in the dim light.

Millie prayed to be invisible even harder as Mistress's eyes swept over the saloon, taking note of Pearl at the piano, of Opal's near nudity, of the grip a card player had on Sapphire's arm, of the way Sterling had his head still close to the man at the bar.

But she was not invisible, because when Mistress's gaze came to rest, it was upon her. Panic snaked down Millie's belly because Mistress was not a stupid woman and there was nowhere else to hide.

Mistress's eyes narrowed, but the look of displeasure was gone when she turned back to look up at a tall, dark man standing next to her. The man bent his head down as Mistress whispered something to him that Millie didn't have a hope of hearing and then he looked up, his gaze locking with Millie's.

She swallowed. He was a large man, and she couldn't tell if his skin was dark from the sun or if he was of mixed parentage. He wore a black duster and a black cowboy hat, which only made him seem more dangerous. His mouth was set in a thin line and his jaw seemed tight. He didn't have the normal gleam of anticipation that so many of the other gentlemen callers did when they walked into the Jeweled Ladies. In fact, he looked rather like she felt—like he might've made a terrible mistake and wished he were anywhere but here.

Then he turned his attention back to Mistress. Millie saw him nod once and then the two of them were making their way toward Millie. In a moment of stark terror, she considered ducking down and hiding behind the bar—but they'd already seen her and besides, Sterling wouldn't shield her.

So she did what she should have done last night. She took a deep breath, straightened her skirts and stepped out into the light. She'd chosen this life. It was time to start living it.

Chapter Two

He shouldn't have come to this place. But a man had needs and Matthew Hawkins was being crushed by the loneliness of his life. Besides, the girl the madam of this brothel was leading him toward was pretty.

No, she wasn't. She was absolutely *stunning*, a vision of gold. The light of the gas lamps made her curly blonde hair glow as if she were an angel and her pale skin was a creamy ivory. She was almost too beautiful—far too fine a lady for the likes of him.

But the madam of this brothel had promised that she had the right woman for him, and Matthew needed a woman. Just for one night. Then he could go back to the ranch and to Jed and, somehow, keep going.

"Miss Gold is a charming young creature," the madam—who had introduced herself as Mistress—was saying as they crossed the saloon. Matthew focused on keeping his stride even. He didn't want to betray a limp now. "I believe you will find her refined and talented. But of course," she went on, "we want you to be happy, so if there's anything else you require, please do not hesitate to let me know." Mistress turned her face up to Matthew and smiled.

She was a pretty lady, too—but there was

something in that smile that made his skin crawl. He was a God-fearing man, although he had not been back to church since his Maria had died. This was a sin and he was probably going to hell, but then—wasn't he already in hell?

Before he could change his mind, they were in front of the girl in gold. Miss Gold. "Topaz, darling," Mistress said. "I would like you to meet Mr. Matthew Hawkins. He is visiting us from a ranch north of Decatur and I believe that you two would be well suited."

Matthew cringed. The woman made it sound like she was a matchmaker, not the proprietor of a whorehouse.

What was he doing here? He wasn't sure he could get his cock to respond if he wanted it to. But just as he opened his mouth to excuse himself from the room—the building—Miss Topaz Gold looked up at him through thick lashes. There was something almost…innocent about her. She really was beautiful and she wasn't making eyes at him like some of the other ladies had done. He got the feeling she wasn't trying to seduce him and somehow, that made this okay. He didn't want to feel like a mark. He only wanted to feel like a man.

He whipped his hat off his head and held it in front of him. "Miss Gold, a pleasure to make your acquaintance."

She gave a little curtsy and his eyes followed her as her body dipped and raised. Compared to what he'd seen some of the other ladies in this building wearing, she was dressed almost appropriately—but there was no missing the creamy swell of her breasts as they surged above the bodice of her dress.

His cock stirred. Good. That was why he was here, wasn't it?

"Mr. Hawkins, I would be honored to spend an evening in your company." Her voice was low and had a husky quality to it that set his blood stirring a little faster. Maybe he could do this. Maybe he could enjoy himself. At the very least, maybe he could just stop thinking for one night.

Mistress squeezed his arm again. "Excellent. Miss Gold, take good care of Mr. Hawkins. And if there's anything else you should need, you know where to find me." Matthew glanced at her to see the older woman giving Miss Gold a harsh look that didn't quite match the gentle lilting tone of her voice.

In reply, he saw Miss Gold swallow hard and then she shot him a smile that was entirely too fake. What flagging interest he had in her disappeared.

He had come here—nearly forty miles away from Decatur—because he'd heard tell that the girls at the Jeweled Ladies were the best in the state—maybe even the country. And what's more, they were all here by choice. No one forced them to do anything. Matthew couldn't bear the thought of taking a girl against her will.

That was why the girls were so expensive. They were trained and ready and willing and, sinner that he was, he was counting on that to push him past his moral reservations and into a place where his animal lusts could take over. Just for tonight. Tomorrow, he would ride back to the Double Bar T branch and get through his life one day at a time.

But if this girl didn't want him—or didn't want to be here—how was he supposed to do any of that?

9

Mistress made purring noise in her throat and then, with a swish of her skirts, she was gone, moving around the saloon like an experienced hostess.

After a moment's hesitation, Miss Gold stepped forward and slid her arm through his. "Hello," she said, as if they had not just been formally introduced. "How are you tonight?"

Matthew could feel the warmth of her body through his coat. He got the feeling that she was trying. Maybe she was just nervous? He could be imposing, he knew that. He was big and dark, thanks to his daddy. He would never be refined and polished, especially not after a hard day's work, when he couldn't help limping and dirt was caked on his skin. He worked for his daily bread and it showed in his hands and face.

Miss Gold barely came up to his shoulder. If any animal lust chose to overcome him at this moment, he could pick her up and throw her over his shoulder with one hand.

Huh. What an odd image. He didn't normally think about women like that.

"Would you like a drink?" she asked and he decided he liked the sound of her low voice, because while she looked like a doll, she sounded like a woman.

"A drink would be appreciated." He was thirty-six years old. He shouldn't need any liquid courage to bed a woman.

But he did.

With just the barest pressure on his arm, she led him to the bar. "Would you like to finish your drink down here or take it upstairs?" The moment the words left her mouth, a great round of shouting broke out at a poker table. The big black man who'd told Matthew he was welcome came barreling through the doors, heading for the fight with his fists ready.

Back home, Matthew would be in there too. He wasn't a lawman, but he valued peace—even when he had to fight for. But this was not his town and these were not his people and he was in no mood to brawl. "I'd rather have some quiet."

He felt her body flutter next to his and he couldn't tell if she was relieved that he wanted to leave the saloon or upset because she wanted to stay.

"What'll you have?" The bartender said, wiping down the counter in front of Matthew.

Matthew ordered a bottle of whiskey and two glasses, although he didn't know if Miss Gold drank spirits or not.

He grabbed the bottle and she took the glasses. "Shall we?" she asked, her voice dancing just over the din of the brawl.

Matthew nodded and let her take the lead. This was fine. He had a bottle of whiskey and a pretty woman and he had all night. Jed was staying with Mrs. MacKay. He needed to do this, needed to get back to where he'd been before his Maria had died. He needed to have something to look forward to besides Jed because, as much as he loved the boy, more and more it felt like that love wasn't quite enough to keep him going.

They climbed several flights of stairs, passing doors where Matthew could hear giggles and moans and shouts. It wasn't until they reached the fourth floor—the very top of the house—that she led him to a

11

narrow doorway. "I'm still new," she said, the apology in her voice, "that's why we're up here."

"You haven't been here long?" There was something almost comforting about that. He wasn't real sure what he was doing. Yeah, he was paying for her experience but he kind of liked that they might be more equal than that.

She started to say something and then closed her mouth and gave him a look that seemed calculated to heat his blood. "Don't worry," she promised, opening the door and standing aside so he could enter. "I know what I'm doing."

It was nice that one of them did. Oh, he knew how to bed a woman. But his wife was dead. It was time to move on.

At least, that's what he told himself.

She lit the lamps as Matthew looked around the room. The room itself was fairly small, but the bed took up most of it. It was the size of bed that he needed but couldn't afford. The covers were neatly turned down and the pillows looked soft and inviting and he felt some of this tension drift away. If nothing else, he'd paid to sleep in that fine bed.

On one side of the bed stood a wardrobe and on the other...

"Is that a wash basin?"

Miss Gold lit the last lamp and turned to face him. "It is. I could draw you a hot bath in this very room, if you'd like."

A hot bath? Not just washing out the pot on the stove? Or out of the ice-cold stream that ran through his property? "I think I'd like that."

He wasn't mistaken this time—she looked

relieved. Maybe she was used to men just throwing her down and having their way with her, but that's not how he was. He couldn't do that if he wanted to—he'd learned with his Marie that he had to take his time and prepare her body for his.

Just because he didn't know Miss Gold well didn't mean he wanted to hurt her.

She moved to the wash basin and turned knobs that were built into the wall. Water began to shoot into the tub and steam began to rise.

Matthew stared at it in amazement. Hot water right from the walls? What would they think of next?

Then she stepped into him and ran her hands over the front of his chest. "Would you like some help undressing?" she asked as she looked up at him through her lashes.

"Yeah," he said, his voice suddenly gruff. Her lips quirked up as her hands slid underneath his coat and pushed it off his shoulders.

"What brings you to Brimstone?" Miss Gold hung his coat on the hook on the door. "We're quite a ways from Decatur, if I'm remembering properly."

"My land is almost forty miles away. I was in town for some…business." Which was kind of true—but mostly he was in town because he didn't want word to get around Decatur that he had taken it upon himself to start visiting whorehouses.

She turned back to him and gave him an appraising look up and down. "I'm honored you've come all this way to be with me."

That made him smile—almost, anyway. She'd seen right through his flimsy excuse. "I'm not ashamed to say it, Miss—I've not done this a lot. I was married, but she died in childbirth almost three years ago."

He didn't know why he told her that. Everyone in Decatur already knew, of course. And he was not looking for sympathy when she flipped up her skirts. But it somehow seemed important that she know that this wasn't a regular, everyday thing for him.

"I'm sorry to hear that," she said in a quiet voice. "I…" she paused and looked down. "It's a hard thing to go on alone, isn't it?"

Warmth bloomed in his chest and it had nothing to do with the way she stepped in and began undoing the buttons on his shirt. The way she'd spoken made it sound like she'd been married—or at the very least, she'd had a sweetheart. Had she lost him in the war? Why else would she be here?

"It is," he agreed, his hands coming to rest on her waist. "You don't think less of me for being here, do you?"

He expected some sort of cooing denial designed to soothe his troubled soul. But that's not what he got. She paused and stared up at him as a wash of emotions flooded her face. Her hands flattened against his chest and he felt his fingers dig into her hips and he knew he needed to hear something from her—not platitudes, not sympathy, but something that was real and honest and truth. Something that told him he wasn't just a cock with cash and she wasn't just a pussy to be fucked.

He wasn't looking for love, not here. But he wanted something more than just animal lust.

"I couldn't," she whispered, lifting a hand to stroke his cheek. It was the sweetest touch he could remember, warmth after a long, cold, never-ending winter. "How could I? I'm here, too. I just…" she took a deep breath. "I don't want you to think less of me for doing this. That's all."

"Why are you here, then?" It wasn't a fair question. A woman had a right to her reasons—and a right to keep them to herself.

"I got tired of depending on someone else to save me," she said, her hand dropping from his face as she turned her attention back to his clothes. "So I decided to save myself. It's a real nice place," she added as she pushed his best shirt from his shoulders and then carefully hung it up. "Better, I think, with you here."

Matthew scoffed at that line—because that's what it was, a line. The ache in his leg seemed to get louder. He looked longingly at the bath. How much longer could he stand? "I don't know if I can do this."

"Take a bath?"

He swallowed. "Bed you. I don't…I don't even know you."

She tilted her head to one side, studying him. "Mr. Hawkins—"

"Matthew." For God's sake, he was half dressed and she was falling out of her gown. He was about to be stripped bare for the luxury of a hot bath—it only seemed right that they know each other's names.

"Matthew," she replied, her tone warm. "I am yours for however long you want me. My bath is yours. My bed is yours. My body is yours. We can talk or be silent, touch or not, have quiet sex under the covers or…" she paused, but kept on, "or loud sex against the wall. If you wanted, I could fetch another girl and you could watch—or join in. If all you want to do is bathe and sleep, I will hold you. We don't have to do a single thing you don't want to do. I will think no less of you, I promise you that."

He scrubbed a hand over his face. When had this seemed a good idea?

"I…" Her voice was low and warm. "I know what it is to be lonely, Matthew. You're a good man, I can tell. So let me take some of that away for you tonight."

He stared at her, a hollowness in his chest. "Just for tonight?"

"I wouldn't ask anything more of you."

Well, hell. He'd come all this way. The basin was half full. He'd brought his money and Miss Topaz Gold was offering him something more than lust.

Companionship. A night that wasn't so quiet.

"All right," he said, holding out a hand to her. "I won't be lonely with you."

He hoped not. She smiled and stepped into him, her breasts brushing against his chest and Matthew hoped he wasn't making the biggest mistake of his life.

Chapter Three

Good Lord, this man was built.

She could feel the heat of his body burning through the clothes as she revealed him, layer by layer. His undershirt went and then his trousers. His chest was the same dark color as his face with a smattering of springy black hair. He didn't even flinch when she plucked at the drawstring on his drawers and shoved them aside.

She gasped as his manhood revealed itself. He was half hard, maybe—but still quite impressive. "Oh, Matthew." What would he look like when he was fully aroused? Would she be able to handle him?

Before the panic could take hold, he slid a finger under her chin and lifted her face until he could look her in the eyes. "Bath first," he said decisively. "And then we'll see what happens. I don't... We'll see what happens," he repeated, sounding none too sure of himself.

She nodded and then, on impulse, leaned up on to her tiptoes and pressed a kiss to his cheek. It was her job to make sure that he was well taken care of. Mistress had told her there would be gentlemen callers like this—lonely widowers who just needed a woman to talk to.

Millie had always envisioned those men as wizened and frail grandfathers who needed someone to tuck them in and spoon them soup. Not unlike her father in his final months.

But Mr. Matthew Hawkins? He was not stooped and frail. He was broad and tall, with hard muscles in his chest and arms. His waist cut in and his legs…

Wait. Was there something wrong with his leg? But before she could ask why he was holding his left leg like that, he asked, "Do you need help with your buttons?"

She turned. It was not her concern if his one leg was misshapen. She was to put him at ease by any means necessary. And if he wanted to undress her, then she was happy to be bared, one button at a time. "If you wouldn't mind?" She could get into and out of the dress on her own. It'd been sewn by Ebony White, another one of the Jewels. All of Ebony's creations were designed for girls to dress and undress themselves quickly.

But fast was not how Matthew Hawkins operated. His large hands moved to the first button and then the next with care. He didn't tear at them or rip the dress. He took his time with her.

There was something intimate about him undressing her as she had undressed him. The room was warm and the sound of the water filling the tub calmed her. Matthew Hawkins was a giant of a man but he was gentle with her and, for that, she was thankful.

The dress gave and she stepped out of it, draping it over the foot of her bed. The tub continued to fill as she lifted the hem of her shift to expose her legs. She didn't say anything as she undid the garter and began to roll down the stocking. Mistress had taught her that some silences were not meant to be filled with chatter. She let Matthew look his fill as she revealed her body for him.

Mistress had spent months training her for this moment and huge bags of money outfitting her with a wardrobe of yellows and golds. She was lucky that her first caller was a kind man. Maybe with a shot of whiskey, they could get through this and both be satisfied.

Satisfaction. Mistress had given her extremely thorough lessons in female pleasure and it hadn't taken long before Millie had realized that her marriage bed had not been satisfying. Not for her, anyway.

She could feel his eyes on her, watching as she revealed inch by inch of her bare legs. She shifted when a strange noise came from where he was standing—a growl. She wasn't wearing drawers and he must've caught a glimpse of her womanhood.

She got the second stocking off and turned to face him. His cock jutted out from the nest of black hair, pointing to her like a divining rod seeking water. He was intimidating—but she took comfort in that sign of physical attraction. She was Topaz Gold, desirable and worthwhile. And she could do this.

She turned her back to him so that he could unlace her stays. Again, she could have done this part by herself but she wanted to feel his hands on her. Would his touch make her shy away? Or would it warm her?

Her stays gave and then, after a moment of hesitation, his big hands reached around her front and undid the busks that held it together. She stared down at where his hands were nimbly slipping metal from metal. His hands were dark against the pale yellow of her corset but there was something undeniably sensual about it.

She held her breath as he pulled the stays away and dropped them on the floor. She didn't move—and for a moment, neither did he. Then his hands touched her high on her ribs, not quite at her breasts. He stroked down, getting the feel of her waist and then lower, moving his hands over her hips and her thighs.

This wasn't how things were to go. She was supposed to be seducing him. But that's not what was happening as he dug his fingers into the hem of her shift and began to pull it up over her body. Because his touch did things to her. A feeling began to churn in her stomach. Logan had never undressed her like this. He never let his hands skim over her body. He hadn't been a violent lover, but for him, she was there to be taken so he took her. There was nothing else to the marriage bed.

She hadn't missed it because what was there to miss?

The shift moved over her hips, exposing the *v* of her womanhood. She let out a shaky breath and lifted her arms so that he could peel the fabric off her. Then she leaned into his touch. An unmistakable warmth spread out from where his rough hands skimmed over her skin. Logan had been rough, too—but not this gentle. In truth, she had been afraid of her husband. And Sterling had never made her feel this warm. Maybe that was why she'd been afraid of this moment. After all, she didn't have the best memories of lying with a man.

But Matthew wasn't Logan. Even where his calluses were hard, they didn't hurt as he ran his hands over the front of her thighs and back up her stomach. Instead of pain, it was…sensation. Awareness. It prickled where he touched her and spread over her entire body.

"You're real pretty," Matthew said in a voice that sounded like gravel. His fingertips traced down her back, going so slow that Millie felt it in her deepest parts. "Real pretty," he repeated as he cupped her backside in his palms.

She could do this. Matthew Hawkins could make her feel womanly and special and she could give him a night where he wasn't alone. Then the sounds of the bath broke through the moment. She needed to turn the water off before she flooded the whole house. She grabbed his hand and led him toward the basin. "Bath first."

He gave her a look and for a moment, she thought he was going to smile. But he didn't. "What about you? I want this to be good for you, too."

A pang of tenderness hit her mid-chest and she almost kissed him again right then and there because she couldn't remember anyone asking what she wanted or would enjoy. Just this lonely cowboy with a bum leg and for that alone, she would give him the world if she could.

But the water was running and he could use a good scrubbing. So instead of throwing her nude body against his, she grabbed the cloth and the bar of expensive French soap that Mistress insisted they use. "Why, sir," she said, batting her eyes at him, "I get to wash you."

The water was, indeed, hot as it lapped over Matthews' thighs. His cock bobbed up and down, more than a little interested now. Miss Gold... Undressing her had been like pushing aside the clouds to reveal a ray of sun.

The tub was more than big enough for him and a little thrill went through him when she stepped into it with him.

He had never done this with his Maria. They'd never had a basin big enough but beyond that, she had been a modest woman and a good Catholic. Matthew had never gotten her stripped to anything more than her shift before she insisted on being under the covers with the candle blown out. He hadn't minded much, though. After he had learned how to warm her body up for his, they'd fallen into a passionate love affair.

God, he missed loving his wife.

It wasn't right to bring his dead wife into this room not with Miss Gold nude and standing over him in the tub. There wasn't much right about his being here but the least he could do was not sully her memory with what was going to happen here.

Besides, the slope of Miss Gold's hips, the smooth roundness of her belly, the long lines of her legs and ankles—and the light brown triangle of curls that covered her sex—she was almost too fine for him.

"How long are you in town?" she asked as she applied the soap and cloth to his legs. She scrubbed him good, and he reveled in the feeling of being clean.

"I head back tomorrow. I can't be gone long." He didn't like leaving Jed, even if Mrs. MacKay doted on the boy. He knew better than anyone that Jed could be a handful.

Miss Gold slid to her knees in the tub, lifting one leg and setting it on the rim of the basin and placing the other in her lap. Where Matthew's ankle rested on her thigh, the water seemed to get much, much hotter. "Do you come this way often?" Maybe it was the hot water, but he swore a delicate blush colored her cheeks.

He almost smiled at that. "No, not often." Was she looking for another visit? And if she was, was that just because his money was good here or because she'd taken a liking to him?

Not that he would hold that against her if she was only interested in his money. His cattle had a good year at market. He could afford the night here.

Something wasn't quite right about her. Not that Matthew had a whole lot of experience with ladies of the night, but he was sure they were supposed to be more sensual and confident, looking to earn a coin and then earn another one.

But not Miss Gold. Oh, she touched him—her small hand curled around his calf as she lifted his leg so she could clean behind his knees. But she didn't seem overly confident. He couldn't quite figure her out.

A comfortable silence descended over them as she washed his good leg. He wanted to relax into this moment but he knew what was coming.

She switched to his left leg. "Do you want to talk about this?" she asked, running her slim hands over the twisted mass that was his calf muscle.

"I apologize for that. I know it's not pretty to look at. You don't have to touch it." He hoped she would take him up on that. Maria had never minded his leg, but then again, she'd never seen or touched it.

"Does it bother you?" Instead of letting loose of his calf, she grabbed the knotted skin and squeezed.

Matthew just about came out of the tub as agony shot through his leg. Water sloshed over the tub as he grabbed at the edge and tried to pull his leg away from her. "Sweet damned Jesus, woman! What the hell are you doing?"

She looked alarmed—but not scared. How was that possible? "I take it that's a yes. What are you doing to treat it?" she asked, as if he hadn't just taken the Lord's name in vain.

"Treat it?" He scowled at her. Hard. But she didn't cringe in fear or anything. She just sat there, looking worried. "I don't need to treat it. It healed."

Damnation. He could get out of this tub and throw his clothes back on and get the hell out of here—which is what he should have done in the first place. But the water felt good and there was no way he could storm away without limping now and...and...

And Miss Gold rested her hand on his shin and somehow it was reassuring, damn it all. And she was still nude and beautiful and the water felt good.

With a noise of disgust, he lowered himself back down into the water, making sure not to splash. "I took a bullet there at Galveston when the Rebs retook the city."

She sucked in a breath and lifted the whole leg by the ankle again. "Ah," she said in a quiet voice. "Here?" She touched a finger to the hole in his leg. Oh, it had healed, but there was a depression of about an inch that he figured would never fill in.

He tensed, but it didn't hurt. "The bullet missed bone and went right through the muscle. The surgeons didn't hack it off with a rusty blade, so that was lucky."

It hadn't been luck at all—Matthew had never lost consciousness. They'd tried to hold him down to take his leg but he'd fought them off until his sergeant had arrived and told the butchers to leave him the hell alone.

It hurt to walk sometimes, but he walked anyway—and rode and chased his son.

She moved to touch the twisted scar again and he tensed. "I won't hurt you again," she said and damn it all, she sounded solemn about it. "I think I can help you."

"How?"

She looked up at him through her lashes and he remembered again that he was in a tub of water with a pretty woman who would let him do anything he wanted to.

So what did he want to do?

Chapter Four

No wonder the poor man had a limp. Millie studied his scar again, trying to see the ways the muscles all connected under the skin.

Millie was not a nurse but after her father had been thrown from his horse, she had learned a great deal about how a man was put together and how to take care of a body when it broke. Her father had needed to have his arm stretched and massaged twice a day or the muscles became painfully knotted, the same with his leg. His valet had worked on Father's leg but Millie had helped with his arm.

Given how Matthew had jumped when she'd given his leg a squeeze, she was willing to bet he was in a great deal of pain.

She looked up at him again and smiled. She might not feel confident she could please him in bed, but this? She could help ease this man's burden.

"Whiskey?" she asked, leaning over and snagging the bottle and the glasses. If she were right and his scarred muscle could be loosened up, it would hurt at first. Quite a lot. But when his muscles relaxed, she thought he would feel immeasurably better.

"Yeah," he said gruffly, watching her breasts as she moved around the tub.

She poured him a large glass and a smaller amount for herself and then settled back in the tub, taking a sip and thinking. If she could make him come, he'd be even more relaxed. She was pretty sure, anyway. Either way, if she turned the conversation back to sex, he wouldn't look at her like she was the Devil incarnate.

She smiled at her own silliness. Yes, she really was going to voluntarily discuss sex. "You could tell me what you like," she offered over the rim of her glass.

Matthew inhaled deeply. "How do you mean?"

She took another ladylike sip of her whiskey and set it down outside the tub. Then she lathered up the cloth again and began to stroke it over his thighs, getting ever closer to his cock.

He really was an impressive specimen of man. Had he had another woman since his wife had passed? Or had he just made due?

Just made due, she decided as she watched his cock harden and lengthen impressively. Mistress had provided her with a small jar of oil that would help her body take in a gentleman's larger member, but Millie hadn't anticipated using it on the first night.

What would he feel like, sliding into her body? Would it hurt, like it had with Logan? Would it be pleasant enough, like it had been with Sterling? Or would there be the release Mistress had described for her? She didn't know.

There was only one way to find out.

She came to her knees. He stared as the water dripped off her nipples and her body responded. Her nipples tightened as she spread her thighs to straddle his legs. Then she applied herself to washing his arms.

27

"Like this," she murmured as his cock nestled against her sex. She shifted her hips but didn't stop lathering up his body. "Do you like this?"

He exhaled hard, staring down at where her breasts were pressed against his chest. "I...my wife," he said, his hips flexing ever-so-slightly, dragging his cock along the folds of her sex. Little sparks of pleasure tingled over her sex at the movement. "I loved her."

She recognized these thoughts—guilt. Mistress had said some men knew they were sinning and it weighed heavily upon them and it was Millie's job to absolve them of their guilt. "I can tell you did. She must have been a wonderful woman," she added as she washed his other arm.

"She never let me see her. We married and then I went to war and then I came back and I loved her," he repeated. "But I never got to watch her undress or keep the lamp lit so I could watch her face, her...her body."

Never? She tried to untangle what he'd said. She knew now many men liked to watch sex acts—their own and others.

It had been wrong and dirty and yet, there'd been something deeply arousing about watching a man's cock slide into a woman's mouth or pussy.

Pressure built low in her body and she shifted her hips again, sending another round of sparks chasing over her skin. "And you could not watch her body taking yours in, then?" She reached down between their bodies and brushed the tip of his cock with her fingertips where it jutted out from her thatch of curls. "You could not see this thick cock of yours sliding into and out of her?"

28

Matthew moaned, a quiet noise deep in the back of his throat and his hands came down on her hips, holding her still. "Miss Gold—tell me your name."

She blinked at him. They were forbidden from giving a gentleman their real names because their pasts did not exist. That rule, Mistress had made clear, was iron-clad. "You know my name."

Then, because it looked like he wanted to argue with her and for once—finally—she was aroused and curious and hopeful that sex was more than it'd been with Logan or Sterling, she kissed him. She cupped his face in her hands and brought her lips down over his and shifted her hips in time with the stroke of her tongue against his mouth and he groaned again, a deep noise in the back of his throat that burned through her like a wildfire.

There was a part of her that was worried about this, about not being good enough or about the pain. But then, she'd never felt this level of anticipation before. Her body was flushed and heavy feeling and, as she wound her arms around Matthew's neck and pressed against his chest, she put those concerns aside.

She wasn't in bed with Logan or Sterling. She was in a bath with Matthew and that made all the difference.

Their mouths met again and again. His callused fingers dug into her hips and then one hand drifted up to cup her breast. She moaned against his lips as his grip tightened, her nipple pointed under his touch.

She was supposed to be here for him but suddenly, she wanted more than a quick fuck and a few dollars.

His mouth moved lower, covering her neck with kisses that made her writhe against him. "I want to

29

watch," he murmured against the swell of her breast. "I want to see everything I do to you."

"Yes," she hissed, arching her back so he could capture her breast with his lips. She gasped as his mouth closed around her sensitive flesh and he began to suckle her. "Oh, Matthew."

His hair was wiry and short, but she still laced her fingers into it and held him to her. Pleasure shot from where his lips worked her down to her sex and ricocheted back up from where his cock rubbed against her in lazy circles.

"You're so pretty," he murmured as he turned his attentions to her other breast.

"And you're so handsome," she told him. He tilted his head back, his brow quirked with doubt. "You are," she repeated, dragging her breasts against his chest. The dark hair there was just as rough as the hair on his head and it felt deliciously sinful against her aching nipples. "I want you."

Doubt was replaced with relief—she'd said the right thing. "Bed?"

She nodded and pushed herself away from him. When she stood, the water sheeted down her body and he stared up at her with naked desire. "Real pretty," he said again, sitting forward to trace her legs with his hands.

She held still for the exploration, concentrating on the sensations he unleashed upon her. The air was cooler than the water—and him—and her skin prickled. She shivered but she wasn't sure if it was the chill in the air or the way he was staring at her body.

Because he was looking his fill. His touch reached the top of her thighs and then he hesitated.

"Go on," she said breathlessly. She spread her legs so he could study her sex. "Please touch me, Matthew."

"Yeah," he said, his voice little more than a growl. Then his fingers were against her, spreading the folds of her sex. "Goldie…"

She smiled at the name. True, Topaz didn't exactly lend itself to being cried out in the throes of passion. "Look at you," she said, balancing carefully to nudge his cock with her foot.

He sucked in a breath, but his gaze never left her. "So pink," he murmured and then, finally, he did touch her. His fingers slid over her slit and up to the little button of pleasure that Mistress had located for Millie. "So perfect."

She braced herself, giving him better access and watching him watch her. "I like it when you touch me like that," she told him as his fingers stroked over her flesh. Mistress had told her she would have to exaggerate or occasionally lie outright to convince a man she enjoyed his attentions, but this?

This was not an exaggeration. Or a lie. Matthew's careful strokes woke her body up from what felt like a long, dark sleep. This was passion—the passion she'd hoped to find in her marriage bed. Passion that led to children, to happiness.

No, no—she'd been warned about this. She was not to confuse lust and desire with love. That was the way to heartbreak for a whore.

Then Matthew shifted and instead of stroking along the outside of her body, a single finger pushed into her pussy. Millie gasped as the sensations exploded in her. There was no pain, not even from his

31

rough callouses. Her body took him in and it was both too much and not enough all at once.

"Yes," she hissed, tilting her hips forward and leaning into his hand. She would chase this pleasure, by God. If she could have this one night with this good man, she could erase all the bad memories of Logan. She could hold her time with Matthew close to her heart. "Oh, God—yes."

"You like that?" It wasn't so much a question and before she could answer it, he slid a second finger into her. "Oh, sweet heavens above," he groaned as he began to pump his fingers into her. "You…you're so hot. So wet around me. You feel amazing, Goldie."

She threw her head back and didn't fight the sounds coming out of her mouth. She gave herself over to this moment and this man.

Her knees started to shake with the effort of holding herself upright and then, when she thought she couldn't take another second of pleasure, he leaned up and pressed his mouth against her button.

Millie gasped and lost her fight to stand. She fell onto him and he grunted in surprise, but the water cushioned her fall. "Sorry," she murmured, embarrassment heating her cheeks. Mistress had instructed her about that act, of course—and she'd watched Sterling kiss Opal like that as well. But all the training in the world hadn't prepared her for the swipe of Matthew's tongue against her swollen flesh.

"It's okay." A smile lit his face and there was something so sweet about that—lust-tinged as it was—that she threw her arms around his neck and kissed him all over again.

They kissed for long, glorious minutes before she

forced herself to pull back. The water was cooling and her need was growing too great. This time, instead of standing so he could touch her, she held out her hand to him.

It took him several moments to get his bad leg under him and climb to his feet, but he never once took his eyes off of her. She grabbed a thick towel and rubbed it over his body as quickly as she could and then he did the same for her. The towel stroked over her skin, rough and exciting.

Then the towel hit the ground and his hands were on her body again. He spun her around and kissed her hard on the lips before guiding her back to the bed. "Wait," she said as he tried to push her down on the bed.

"Wait?"

She slipped out from underneath him and opened the doors of her wardrobe. The insides of the doors were lined with mirrors and she adjusted them so Matthew would be able to watch himself from the bed.

The moment he realized what she was doing, he leaned onto the bed and groaned. "Goldie, I can't wait any longer. It's been so long…"

She hurried to him and kissed him again. Finally, she dared touch his cock. The massive thing filled her palm so completely that she barely got her fingers wrapped around his girth.

"How do you want me?" she breathed into the crook of his neck as she gripped him and stroked. Heat flooded her pussy when he moaned into her hair. "Take me, Matthew. However you want me, that's how I want you." Then she squeezed the tip of his cock.

What was left of his self-control snapped, apparently, because the next thing Millie knew, he'd spun her around and bent her over the edge of the bed. She made a little squeak of surprise as the panic threatened to roar to life but she didn't fight him. That, at least, had been a lesson worth learning at Logan's hands.

There was no burst of white-hot pain that near tore her in half. Instead, Matthew filled her backside with his hands, squeezing and lifting her flesh apart so he could better see her most private areas.

Millie turned her head to the side and caught sight of them in the mirrors. She tried to remember what she'd been trained to do, but it was hard to think about Mistress's rules and advice when Matthew's hands spread her legs wider. She arched her back, bringing her bottom up into the air.

"Look at you," he said, his voice barely a hoarse whisper. Then he set his fingers against her slit again, rubbing all along the folds of her flesh.

"You feel so good," she told him, pushing back into his touch as his fingers entered her again. "I like that."

She watched him in the mirror. His gaze was fastened upon where their bodies were joined, his thick cock getting closer and closer to her as his hips thrust in time with his hands.

"Matthew," she gasped when he withdrew his fingers and drew her own moisture over her sex. "Please."

"Gotta make sure you're ready," he growled, then he leaned down and bit her on the bottom.

"Matthew!" But it hadn't hurt, not when his fingers slid inside her again. The surprise of pain quickly turned warm and made her grind back against him. "Oh, God," she moaned, burying her face in the bedclothes as everything in her body tightened. She felt her pussy grip his fingers and he made a noise of raw lust that pushed her to a place she'd never even glimpsed before.

"So wet for me," he growled and then, just as her tension was beginning to break, he pulled his hand away.

She whimpered but then he fit the head of his cock against her. She braced for the invasion, but he didn't slam into her. Instead, he reached over and grabbed her by the hair, bringing her head up and forcing her back against his cock. "I need you so bad," he moaned in her ear, "but I don't want to hurt you. If it's too much, tell me to stop and I will."

Dear God, she was not to confuse love with lust but when he said things like that, when he took the time to prepare her body for his—how could she not fall a little in love with him? Because this was raw and needy and yet still ripe with tender sweetness.

Had she ever had sweetness before? No. No, she had not.

"Okay?" he demanded. "You'll tell me if it's too much?"

"Yes," she hissed, pushing back against him. "But make me yours, Matthew. Now."

He grunted and let go of her hair. Both his hands gripped her bottom, spreading her wide as he began to thrust into her.

Millie's breath caught in her throat as her body struggled to take his in, but Matthew went slow, giving her time to adjust to his girth. She was able to breathe through the initial discomfort and when she did, her body widened for his.

"God," he said and it didn't sound like blasphemy. It sounded…like a prayer.

She fisted the bedclothes as he thrust again and was fully inside of her. "You're so big," she moaned, shifting her hips to better tuck him inside her pussy. "But you feel so very good."

"So pretty," he ground out and then he began to thrust. Slowly at first but it wasn't long before he set a rhythm that had her crying out each time he buried himself deep inside her.

And Millie? She was a shameless, brazen hussy underneath him. In the mirror, she watched him fuck her, watched him watching himself as he pounded into her. She could just see his cock, slick with her juices, when he pulled out before he buried himself inside of her again and again and heaven help her, it was the most erotic thing she'd ever seen.

She moaned and cried out and ground back onto him every time he thrust into her. God, it had never been like this with her husband. This was what she'd wanted when she'd run away to be a mail-order bride—this raw hunger, this passion. If only Matthew had ordered her instead of Logan…

The pleasure spiraled out of control and her body seized up on her. She cried out her crisis, muffling her scream in the mattress. Behind her, Matthew grunted again and gripped her by the hips and slammed into her two more times before a roar broke free from his chest.

She looked up in time to glimpse the look on his face—his eyes squeezed tight, his mouth open—before he pulled free of her body and spurted his climax onto her back. Then he went limp, falling onto her and pinning her to the bed with his hot body.

They lay there, panting hard. This wasn't how it was supposed to be. Mistress had told her she might not shatter like this, certainly not every time. And she was absolutely not to develop feelings for her gentlemen callers, no matter how tender or sweet or simply good in bed they were.

Especially not ones who lived forty miles away, who she might not ever see again.

Matthew reached up and covered her hand with his, lacing their fingers together. No, Millie wasn't supposed to fall for him.

But what if it were already too late?

Chapter Five

Sweet Jesus!" Matthew did his best not to kick because if he did, he knew he would catch Goldie with his heel and he didn't want to hurt her.

Especially not after what they shared in this bed. He had dreamed of taking his Maria like that, dreamed of watching his cock slide in and out of her body. And truthfully, it had been everything he had ever wanted it to be, maybe even more. The only thing he would've changed was that he wished it had been Maria.

Well, that and his leg not cramping up on him.

"Hold still," Goldie said. Seconds later, what felt like metal spikes dug into his scarred leg.

He couldn't keep from cursing, so he buried his face in her pillow in some attempt to preserve her ears. It went on and on, the stabbing pain and for a moment, at the worst of it, he was sure she was cutting into him with an actual knife.

Then, abruptly, the stabbing sensation faded away. His leg felt hot and strange, but bearable.

"There," she said, sounding satisfied. When he felt her lips pressed against his shoulder, he lifted his head from the pillow. "That wasn't so bad, was it?"

Matthew gave her a dull look. "Goldie, there isn't enough whiskey in the world for this."

He liked that little smile on her face. He couldn't be intimate with a woman he couldn't call by her first name and he couldn't bring himself to call her Topaz. What kind of name was that?

The nickname seemed a good compromise. And she did shimmer like gold. "Would you like another shot of whiskey? We still have half a bottle."

He nodded, rolling onto his side and lifting his scarred leg up. There were no puncture wounds, no blood flowing. He ran his hand over the scar tissue. His skin was hot to the touch and slick with some sort of oil, but amazingly, it didn't hurt as much as he expected it to after what she'd done. He could even flex his foot without pain—almost. "What did you do?"

She turned, and his gaze was drawn back to her body. Neither of them had put on clothing after their romp on the bed. There was something so freeing about a woman who wasn't ashamed of her body. A woman who would let him watch.

She leaned forward, her generous breasts shifting. "It never healed right. I can tell that. You won't believe me, but all I did was massage the scar tissue."

He took the glass of whiskey and downed half of it. The burn pushed back against the lingering pins and needles in his leg. "You're right, I don't believe you."

She took another sip of her own whiskey and then picked up a small glass jar. She unscrewed it and dipped her fingers inside. They came out shiny with oil. "I'm going to give you this," she told him, screwing the lid back on. "And I want you to promise me that when you get back home, you will do this."

Before Matthew could ask what, she picked up

39

his leg and held it so his foot was flat against her stomach, his toes almost nestled between her breasts. "I don't think I can do this part without you," he said, wiggling his toes.

She laughed, her voice low and sensual. "No, not that—this." Then she rubbed her slick fingers along the side of his leg, made a C shape with her hand and stroked up and down his calf while squeezing.

"Dammit," he howled. "What's that supposed to help?"

"If you don't work your muscles loose, they're going to freeze in this position for the rest of your life. You'll slowly lose the ability to walk and, I daresay, ride." She squeezed his muscles again. This pain still spiked, but it wasn't as severe this time. Then she took his foot and flexed it back and forward and he was stunned to see it move much more than he could ever do on his own. "See?"

"Are you a nurse?" There'd been a lot of nurses running on the edge of battlefields. Maybe she'd even treated him.

But even as the thought occurred to him, he knew it wasn't possible. He would've remembered her.

She shook her head. "My father..." She pulled up short and turned to take another sip of her whiskey. "I've treated conditions like this before, but I'm not a nurse."

Matthew finished his drink and lay back on the bed. The pillows were soft under his head and the sheets free of dust. His skin was clean and his mind was almost clear. His worries would still be there in the morning but right now, he could put them aside because of this woman.

40

He patted the bed next to him and was pleased when she settled in the crook of his arm. "You were going to tell me something about father, weren't you?"

"It doesn't signify," she told him, tracing small circles around his nipple. "We're not supposed to talk about our lives before we came here," she added in a much quieter voice, as if she were afraid someone would overhear her. "It's one of the rules."

"I won't tell. But I'd sure feel better about you poking and prodding me if you knew what you were doing."

She sighed, flattening her hand on his chest. "My father was in a terrible riding accident that left half of his body mangled. His valet and I worked with him constantly to keep his left side from seizing up. If we stretched and massaged his muscles twice a day, he could even walk for short distances. But if we didn't, he was in agony."

It had been three years since he'd been shot in the leg and not once did he think to stretch out the muscles. Instead, they had just gotten tighter and he'd gotten more crippled.

Then he thought about the other thing she said. Her father was a man of means, one rich enough to have his own servants. Had the valet been a slave? Or a paid employee? He didn't want her to have been on the Confederate side.

If she wasn't supposed to talk about her past, he didn't think he'd find out.

"If you can, try to work the muscles loose every evening before you sleep," she went on. "It'd be best if you did it at the beginning and end of the day, but once is a good start. If you do it regularly, it'll help."

41

What the hell. "I will," he promised. It was worth a shot because she was right—slowly, he been losing what little ability he had to walk without pain.

They were quiet, although it was comfortable silence. Matthew skimmed his hand up and down her shoulder and back while she stroked his chest. It felt so good to have a woman in his arms again. Yeah, some of that was because bedding her had been amazing. But he'd missed this, missed it dearly. He and Maria had always lain in bed, catching up on their day before they slipped off to sleep with their arms around each other. Even when they hadn't done anything more than kiss good night, there had been a closeness that he hadn't realized how much he needed until it was gone.

Goldie pushed herself up onto her elbow and stared down at him. "How long can you stay? I know a whole night costs a lot of money, but…"

He had twenty dollars that he'd saved up for this. Normally, that would last him a month, almost two. Here, that was a night and a bottle of whiskey.

But it had been worth it already. He got a hot bath from pretty lady and had the kind of sex he'd only fantasized about—plus, she'd helped him with his leg. He considered that money well spent. "I can stay a while longer." Besides, he'd like to have her again. This night was going to have to last him a long time.

She grinned, looking relieved. But then her gaze sharpened and she ran her tongue along her lower lip. Need spiked in his cock at the sight. "Did you see everything you wanted to last time?" As she asked, she slid a leg across his hip and straddled him.

She had such a nice breasts, full and heavy with rosy nipples the size of silver dollars. From this angle, her breasts hung close to his face, practically begging him to lick and suck them.

"This is a pretty good view," he told her, splaying his hands along her back and pushing her down so he could wrap his lips around that nipple and suck until she was squirming against him, until his cock was heavy for her again.

"Oh, Matthew," she sighed in pleasure as he slid along the folds of her sex. "I..." But she swallowed down whatever else she was going to say as he lifted her hips and his cock sprang to meet the entrance of her body.

She was in control this time, deciding how fast she took him in. She was not as slow or patient as he had forced himself to be.

She sank down on him until he was buried inside of her and the pleasure was overwhelming. She sank her fingers into his hair and held him against her breast, where he pulled on her nipple until it was a tight point that rolled over his tongue. She tasted so good, clean and with a hint of lavender. Yes, he knew it was the soap, but it combined with her skin to make a musky perfume that filled his senses.

He had missed this so much. He knew it wasn't the same. No one could ever replace his Maria. This was a poor shadow of intimacy, a pale imitation of love. But it was better than the nothing it had been for almost three years. And so he let himself sink into the glory of it all every time he sank into her body.

But he needed to see more. He relinquished her breasts and leaned back, watching where her body came down on his again and again. If he had thought there couldn't be anything better than watching his dark cock bury itself in her pink pussy while he grabbed at her bottom, then he hadn't anticipated this. She was right on top of him, right surrounding him. Her tight heat gripping him, her moans in his ears, her scent on his tongue—it was *all* right.

He was right, for the first time in years. Everything was going to be just fine.

She laced her fingers with his and held herself upright so that he could see the way her breasts bounced with each movement. And her face—he could see her expressions, all bathed in the soft glow of the gas lamps. And somehow, that was even more sensual because her mouth was open and she was breathing hard, her color high, her eyes glazed with desire.

He was a lot to take in, he knew that. Hawkins men were big and Maria, bless her heart, hadn't been able to handle it. But this woman? This gorgeous and delicate lady who wasn't disgusted by his scar or by him—she rode him like he was a prize stud.

Oh, how he bucked and thrust and held on for the ride of his life. This was what he'd needed—one night where he didn't worry about Jed and mourn the loss of his wife. Or the loss of his manhood. One night where the war had never happened and death wasn't his constant companion. One night to feel alive again.

It wasn't too much to ask, was it? He hoped not.

The tight glove of her body drew down on him and she threw back her head to cry out, "Matthew!" In that moment he couldn't hold anything back. He followed her over the edge to oblivion, barely pulling her off his cock before he let loose.

He made a right proper mess of his stomach and her bed, but that was okay, too. He didn't want to risk getting her with child because he knew exactly how risky that was and he didn't want to do anything that would hurt this woman. Not after this gift she'd given him.

Even if they never had anything else but this night, he wanted all of her memories of him to be good because he knew that they would be some of his most cherished treasures—his, and his alone. No one else but Goldie would ever know what they'd done here.

She fell forward on his chest and his arms came around her back and held her tight. "Oh, Matthew," she said, sounding all happy and that made him happy because he was still a man and he could do this for a woman.

He didn't know how long they lay like that, but he was in no hurry to move. His body was heavy and relaxed—even his leg felt good. He could stay here all night.

But eventually, they had to move. Goldie peeled herself off him and went to get the cloth out of the tub. The water had cooled but he didn't mind as she cleaned them. Perhaps it wasn't the gentlemanly thing to let her do that, but he didn't have much energy left. He was used to crushing exhaustion, but this was the good kind of tired.

He held out his hand to her and was thrilled when she curled against his side once again. She pulled the covers up over them, which he took as permission to stay and rest for a while.

"I want to tell you something," she said, her voice barely a whisper. "You are my first caller here."

He struggled to get his eyes open. She'd said she was new, right? But Mistress hadn't promised him a virgin and she certainly hadn't acted like one. Maria had been a virgin and although he'd been as careful as he could've, he'd still hurt her. "Not your first ever, though, right?" Guilt suddenly swamped him. But her cries—they hadn't sounded pained. She hadn't bled. And she'd happily taken him a second time.

She shook her head against his shoulder and he let out a breath. "I was married. It didn't last long before he died. I wound up here. Matthew, I'm glad you are my first caller." Her arms tightened around him. "More glad that you can know."

His chest swelled with pride. He had not been selfish and he had not used her poorly. It was possible she was just saying that because it was what she was supposed to say, but he didn't think so.

He wished he could be her last, too. But the moment the thought crossed his mind, he shook it away. This was not permanent and he'd be a fool to start thinking like that. "I'm glad to have been your first here," he told her as he kissed her on her forehead.

"Will you come back?" she asked, sounding impossibly young. "I know it's a long way, but I'd like to see you again."

Yes. But he didn't say that, not out loud. Just because this was one of the best nights in the last three years of his life didn't mean he could ignore reality and the fact was, it would take him several days to get home and he couldn't spend all his money here. He had to see to his and Jed's future. The boy had to come first. "I'd like that too, but I can't be sure. I can't leave my son much."

"How old is he?"

"Gonna be three in a few months." Matthew chuckled. "He's a handful, let me tell you. Just like I was at that age."

"Tell me about him," she said, burrowing further into his side.

So he did. He told her about how Maria's pregnancy had been hard from the beginning and how Jed had been too big for her and she'd lost too much blood, how his neighbors had given him a goat so he could feed the baby. He told her about the long nights while Jed teethed and hiring a neighbor's wife to wash the baby's diapers and how most days, he went to bed wondering how on earth he'd get up the next day and do it all over again, but then Jed would smile or say "Da" for his first word and it'd all be okay for a little bit longer.

And she listened the whole time, asking questions and laughing when he told her about Jed licking a turtle he'd found because they had turtle-shell bowls.

"You need a wife, Matthew," she told him later as he drifted in and out of sleep. "You're a good man and a good father. Why aren't you married?"

He didn't want to tell her it was because he was ashamed of his leg, of the pitying looks the eligible widows in Decatur gave him across the aisle at church. Besides, those weren't the only reasons to avoid women. "I was married," he told her simply. "And it was my fault she died. I got her with child and it killed her."

"Oh, Matthew," she said, holding him tight.

Neither of them said anything else. An hour later, when Goldie's breathing was steady and her body was twitching with sleep, Matthew slipped out of her bed and dressed as quietly as he could.

47

He knew what she'd been implying—that she might be a good wife. She liked him well enough and they'd fit together real good.

But he hadn't lied to her. It was his fault that Maria was dead and Matthew simply wasn't going to risk the life of another woman he cared about.

He wanted to kiss her goodbye, a perfect, sweet ending to the best evening he could remember. But he had miles to go and a little boy waiting on him and besides, goodbyes weren't his favorite things.

She was so beautiful, though, with her hair all spread out on the pillow. He tucked the memory of her like this away in his mind and then he walked out of her room and out of the brothel.

It was a hell of a lot harder than he expected it to be.

Chapter Six

One month later

Matthew stood in the doorway to the saloon, wondering if he was making another mistake.

Because it'd been a mistake to come to this brothel last time, of that he had no doubt. Because it was supposed to have been an evening with Miss Gold. One night where he could be a man—not a widow, not a father, not a cripple. Just a man.

That night in her arms had haunted him for the last month. Goldie was with him when he was working cattle, tempting him when he made dinner for Jed and haunting his dreams when he finally fell into bed at the end of another exhausting day.

He flexed his foot—something he was still get used to doing. When he'd run out of that fancy oil she'd given him, he resorted to using bacon grease— but it was worth it. Even after a long day, his pain was significantly less and he had her to thank for that, too.

Not that she would even remember him. A month was a long time, especially when she probably took two or three men to her bed every night. If she were even still here. There was always a chance she could have moved on and if she had…

Well. If she had, then he'd be able to save his money. He'd sold off a few extra cows he hadn't planned on to afford this trip down to Brimstone and he didn't want to waste his money. He only wanted Goldie.

The saloon was crowded tonight and at first, he didn't see her. But then, just when he was about to despair, she lifted her head. She was hanging over the back of a poker player, her arms around his neck and her breasts pressed against his shoulder. Something had changed about her, Matthew could tell. She wasn't hiding in the corner anymore. For some ridiculous reason, that saddened him.

Then she saw him. For the longest second, they just stared at each other and Matthew knew he had made a fool of himself because either she didn't remember him or she wasn't glad to see him. He didn't know which one would be worse

Slowly, she straightened, pulling away from the gambler. Then everything changed all at once. She clasped her hand in front of her and the biggest smile broke out over her face. He couldn't hear her, but he saw her lips move and he hoped like hell she was saying his name.

And then she was running toward him, laughing and crying "Matthew!" and this time he heard her, loud and clear. As she made her way around the tables and the gamblers and the other soiled doves. She ran right to him and threw her arms around his neck and said, "Oh, Matthew, you came back," and damned if Matthew didn't hear a hitch in her voice, as if she were trying not to cry.

He picked her up and slung her around, savoring

the feel of her in his arms again. For all his thinking about her, *this* was what he'd been missing. His blood pounded in his veins with want and need. "I couldn't stay away," he told her and then he kissed her, not caring who saw them. He'd spent every day of the last month thinking about kissing her. He wasn't going to waste a second of their time.

Someone behind him hooted as he set her down, but he ignored them. The only person he could see was Goldie. "I wasn't sure you'd remember me."

She gave him a look of such indignation that he couldn't help but smile like he was still a boy and it was Christmas morning. "As if I could forget," she said, smacking him on the arm. "Do you want to drink? Or…"

He shook his head. "I don't want anything but you."

The way her whole face lit up—it did things to them that had nothing to do with his cock and everything to do with his heart because she had missed him. The hardness around her eyes faded and she sure as hell looked happy he'd come back.

He swept her up into his arms, cradling her against his chest as he turned and made for the stairs. He almost knocked over some dandy and the lady in deep green as he took the stairs two at a time, but he didn't care. He had his Goldie back in his arms and everything was right again.

His leg was better but he'd forgotten how many stairs were in this house. "Remind me why you're on the top floor?" he playfully grumbled when he had to set her down at the bottom of the third staircase.

"How's your leg?" She took a step back and looked him up and down.

51

No, she hadn't forgotten him at all. It made him ridiculously happy, that. "Much better, thanks to you." He let her lead the rest of the way up. But he couldn't keep his hands off her body. This was a different dress, although it was just as pretty. The skirt was shorter and he could catch glimpses of her ankles. He caught hold of the hem, lifting it up so that he could see her shapely calves.

Heat flamed through his body as he caught flashes of her creamy skin. She wasn't wearing drawers—again. When he traced a finger over her leg, she giggled and slapped his hand away. "Almost there," she told him, her voice breathless.

He didn't think it was just the stairs.

Then they were at her room. The moment she got the door shut behind them, he pulled her against his chest and kissed her hard. It didn't seem possible that he had missed her this much. He had gone without a woman for years before her—but this was different. She was different—or maybe it was him.

Because the man that had married Maria Fernandez would not pick a woman up and practically throw her onto a bed. Nor would he flip up her skirts while she grabbed at the buttons of his trousers. And he certainly wouldn't pause only long enough to open up the wardrobe doors so that he could watch how wicked he was about to be.

She spread her legs wide for him, a matching grin on her face as he stared down at the petals of her sex. "I missed you so much," she said as she grabbed him by the shirt and pulled him down. She wrapped her legs around his waist and then he was against her. He had a fleeting thought that he was doing this wrong—

he hadn't prepared her. But she lifted her hips and the tip of his cock slid inside her and that was the last thought he had for a while. She was tight and wet and although she gasped when he thrust inside of her, it didn't seem like pain. She moaned against his mouth and then kissed him again and again before pushing him away and saying, "See what you do to me?"

And he did. He grabbed at the low-cut bodice of her gown and pulled it down even further, revealing her tight nipples. He pinched one and then turned his attention to where he was sliding in and out of her, sliding harder and harder while she cried out her pleasure. She took his hand and guided it down over the curls that covered her sex and pressed his thumb against a little nub. "Here," she moaned, thrashing her head when he pressed down.

With his other hand, he pushed her knee back, opening her even wider. His cock was slick with her juices when he pulled out and sliding back into her was the sweetest thing he'd ever known. He needed this—he needed her.

She clutched at his arms, her fingernails grabbing for purchase. "Matthew—oh, God!" she cried out. Her back came off the bed as her body tightened around his.

"Mine," he growled as she gripped him with such force that he almost didn't withdrawal quick enough. He almost didn't want to. If he got her with child, then he'd have good reason to take her away from here. Because she'd be his, not anyone else's.

His instincts screamed at him to bury himself to the hilt and let loose but at the last second, he remembered his wife, screaming and bleeding and then, once the baby was out, there wasn't any more screaming. Just bleeding.

He couldn't do that to his Goldie. He couldn't do it to any woman.

He jerked back, spurting his seed all over her legs and her dress, but it was a close thing. He'd almost stayed inside of her. He'd almost risked her. His chest was heaving and he wanted to do something he hadn't done in years—run.

"Matthew?" She asked in a careful voice as she leaned up on her elbows. "Are you okay?"

He scrubbed a hand over his face, trying to get his mind to work again. He hadn't even gotten his boots off before he'd taken her. "Goldie…" He turned away from her and righted his clothes. He heard rustling, so he assumed she was doing the same.

What was wrong with him? He'd spent a month dreaming of this moment and now it was here and he couldn't even think straight. Even after he'd gotten his buttons done up, he couldn't bring himself to turn around and face her because he wasn't sure what he was going to do.

She was his but he couldn't have her. How did that make any sense at all?

And then it didn't matter because she stepped next to him, sliding her arm around his waist. She just leaned into him and that was what he needed. He wrapped an arm around her shoulders and held her tight.

"Millie," she said, her voice barely a whisper.

"What?"

She looked up at him, her eyes shining. "My name is Millie."

Chapter Seven

M illie Townsend," Millie said, sinking back into the bath water. She wasn't supposed to tell him this. No one was supposed to know. But the weight of a month of being Miss Topaz Gold wore heavy on her and if she didn't tell someone who she was, how badly she'd erred—then she'd just keep dying a little more every day.

She stared at the man between her legs. Matthew Hawkins had come back for her and that made her chest tight with happiness. It wasn't like he was the first man to return to her bed because he wasn't. She'd picked up a regular hired hand from a nearby ranch and she thought that Rev. Mays might come see her again, too.

That was normal, Mistress had told her. Men took comfort in the familiar.

But she didn't feel this bubbling of hope when the others came back. Her throat closed up with dread, not relief, when the rancher appeared in the saloon. And the thought of the Methodist minister fucking her again made her stomach sick.

But this? Matthew lifted her left leg and set it upon his broad shoulder so that he could scrub her calf, behind her knees, her inner thigh. This wasn't just comfort and it wasn't just relief.

For the first time in a long month, she felt like there was a little light in her life. If Matthew came to see her every so often, she could grit her teeth and get through the rest.

"It's a pretty name," he said in that gruff manner of his as the washcloth dipped closer to her pussy.

"It's not mine. I was only Millie Townsend for a week and a half before my husband got kicked in the head by a mule."

Matthew quirked an eyebrow at her, which was almost the same as anyone else laughing out loud. "That's a right stupid way to die."

She allowed herself a little smile. "I don't think he was a very smart man, may he rest in peace." Nor would Logan have ever sat in a bath and washed his virginal wife to put her at ease.

Millie wasn't lying to herself. She knew that, from this angle, Matthew had quite a view of the folds of her sex. And he couldn't stop staring at how the water lapped at her breasts. He wasn't suffering on her behalf. But she couldn't dismiss the sweetness of this gesture. Certainly none of her other gentleman callers had even thought of doing this.

If there was one thing Millie craved, it was a little sweetness in her life.

"Who were you before you got married?"

She absolutely should not be telling him this. The only other person who knew this was Mistress—and only then because Millie had needed the protection that Mistress promised with a new name and a new life. The more people who knew, the greater the risk that word would trickle back to George and he'd fetch her back to Massachusetts.

But just then, Matthew turned his head and pressed a kiss to the sole of her foot and Millie heard herself say, "Millicent Reynolds."

"That's a big name," he said, lowering her clean leg into the water and lifting up the other. "Sounds important."

"It was, in Boston," she sighed, resting her head back against the back of the tub. Her chest felt lighter for having the truth out there.

"You have family?"

"I did. I guess I still do, if you can count my half-brother as family. My father was a banker."

She waited for the questions about how much money she must have in an account—which did exist. She hadn't been able to figure out how to withdraw the money without alerting George. It hurt that she was screwing half of Texas to earn her keep when she had a thousand dollars with her name on it in Massachusetts.

But Matthew didn't ask about money. Instead, he surged forth, fitting more neatly between her legs, his cock bobbing along in the water. Millie eyed it with interest. It wasn't so different from any other cock— she now had enough experience to make that observation. But it felt different when he was inside of her. He was big, but instead of tearing into her and suffocating her under his weight, he filled her and sheltered her with his body.

Even tonight, when he'd all but thrown her down on the bed and fucked her hard, it hadn't been an assault. It'd been hot and sensual and the most erotic coupling of her life.

Maybe she was lying to herself. The first time he'd been here, she'd had an air of innocence and

57

virtue and he'd liked that about her—because it had matched him. They'd been close to equals that first time, both widowed and struggling to find their way forward.

But she wasn't innocent anymore and her virtue was a dim memory. When he'd left her, Matthew had gone home to his land and his son and done an honest day's work. And Millie?

She'd flipped up her skirts for whoever had a few dollars and a hard cock.

"How did you get from Millicent Reynolds to Millie Townsend?" he asked as he began to stroke the cloth over her stomach and her waist and bless him, he didn't sound like he was judging her. He'd be well within his rights to do so—but that wasn't who he was.

Outside of her father, Matthew Hawkins was the most decent man she'd ever known.

She relaxed into his touch, letting it and the bath water warm her skin. "I saw what was coming. When my mother came from England to marry my father, George—that's my half-brother from Father's first marriage—never forgave either of them. When I came along, it only made things worse." Which was as nice a way as she could figure to say that George had hated her with a burning passion.

"Doesn't seem fair to you," Matthew remarked, his voice almost too calm. "You were just a baby and he was how old?"

"Thirteen years older than me." And bitter and vindictive and cruel.

She'd tried so hard not to hate George. It wasn't Christian and he was family. But he made it so difficult to turn the other cheek, controlling everything about the household. "After Father was thrown from his horse, he was never the same. It took him another three years to die, but while he was still alive, he protected me and our hired help. We never owned slaves," she added because Matthew was watching her closely.

"Ah." That was all he said, but it was clear he was relieved.

George had taken control of the family funds. Still grieving for her father's injuries, Millie had suddenly found herself without pin money—or any money at all. She'd had to beg for the coin to put food on the table. The servants had held on for as long as they could out of loyalty to Father, but loyalty didn't put bread on the table.

"Right sorry for your loss, Millie." He said her name intentionally and she smiled. She'd be willing to bet a night's wages that, in at least one corner of his mind, she would always be Goldie.

"Thank you, although I've accepted it as God's will. I did my best. I went from a pampered—some might say spoiled—child to suddenly doing all the cooking and cleaning and washing, as well as tending to Father. And then when he died, it became clear very quickly what George had in mind for me. For the first time in a number of years, I got a new dress. Friends of his started coming around, leering at me. And I knew. I just *knew* that he was going to sell me off."

Matthew paused, staring at her. "But you wound up here?"

"My choice," she pointed out. "At least..." she swallowed and dropped her gaze. "It's not a good choice, but it was still mine to make."

He appropriated her arm for the bath. "Go on."

"I never did figure if George wanted the money or if he were punishing me for existing, but it didn't matter. I couldn't stay and take whatever hell he was preparing for me. I read an advertisement in the paper for a bride, a woman to cook and clean and raise a family and I—"

"Wait," Matthew interrupted, letting go of her hand so fast that it splashed water everywhere. "You were a mail-order bride?"

She nodded. "I wasn't raised as a ranch hand, but I figured it couldn't be any harder than what I'd done for Father. And at the very least, it'd put me beyond George's reach."

Matthew was still staring at her, his mouth open and his eyes wide. What on earth? How could he not even blink an eye at her being a whore but the idea that she'd married a stranger out of necessity was somehow shocking?

"He made me feel powerless, Matthew," she explained, because she didn't like shocking him. Not like this. "He took away my life and I'll be damned if I let him have it back. So I ran away to Texas. I married Logan Townsend within an hour of meeting him at the train depot and gritted my teeth through the week and a half of marriage. His family held on to me until it became clear that I wasn't expecting a Townsend baby and then they had the marriage annulled. I had nothing. *Again*." She couldn't stop the bitterness from tainting her words sour.

It shouldn't upset her. These were the facts and there was nothing she could do now to change them. There was no point in getting teary over her past again, either—especially not while Matthew was here. They had so little time together and she felt the fool for wasting it by pouring out her sob story.

His hands were resting on her thighs now as he stared at her in open concern. This was why Mistress didn't want the girls to talk about their histories because the focus was supposed to be the gentlemen. They didn't pay to have sex with someone who was pitiful. Pity was never erotic.

"I kept Logan's name because I can't risk George finding me. It's why I'm here," she went on, unable to take the weight of his gaze any longer. "Mistress is sheltering me. She gave me a new name and new clothes, a chance to earn my place. I..." Her throat caught.

"Millie."

The tenderness in his voice almost undid her, so she didn't let him talk. "She said that after a couple years, I'd have enough money that I could do whatever I wanted. I wouldn't ever have to rely on anyone again." Her voice broke, but she couldn't look at him. "That's why I'm here. That's why I've stayed, even though..."

He slid a hand under her chin and raised her face and she had no choice but to look into his big brown eyes. The caring that she saw there—it nigh onto broke her heart. Because aside from her father, no one else had cared for her. Not like Matthew did. She had been a means to an end, nothing more.

That wasn't how Matthew made her feel. God help her for that.

"Millie," he said again, with more force. His hand cupped her cheek, a gesture of such tenderness that her eyes filled with tears.

"Yes?"

"Marry me."

The words tumbled out before Matthew knew that he was going to say them. But now that they were out there, he couldn't take them back. He didn't want to.

He wasn't sure what he expected Millie—Millicent—to do. Throwing her arms round his neck and saying *yes* would've been great. He could pull her out of this tub, button her back into that pretty dress and walk her out of here within a quarter of an hour.

But she didn't. Instead, she clutched his hand to her cheek, her eyes filling with tears and it hurt him more than he thought it would. "I can't," she said, her voice little more than a whisper.

"Why not?" Because the more he thought about it, the more sense it made. "I like you. I like you a whole lot. I haven't been able to stop thinking about you for the whole month. I need a wife. I've got a son who needs a mother. If you were willing to marry some stranger, why not me?"

She dragged in a shaky breath but didn't say anything.

Damn, damn, damn. He should have kept his mouth shut—or at least waited until she wasn't already upset. If he ever met her brother—well, Matthew owned a nice piece of land. No one would be able to find a shallow grave.

She looked like he'd slapped her—and he couldn't stand that. He tried again. "You know I'd treat you right, Millie. We get on great together, don't we?" He wasn't sure if he was begging or not.

If he thought that was going to make things better, he thought wrong. Her tears fell faster. Then—and only then—did she throw her arms round his neck. He folded her in his arms, her breasts pressing against his chest. She was shaking, damn it all. "Oh, Matthew—if I could, I would walk out of here with you right now."

"Then let's leave. Let's get dressed and go. We'll get out of town and then we'll get married and you won't have to worry about your brother or this brothel ever again." She had to say *yes* because he couldn't leave her terrified and upset like this. He couldn't leave her for another man to use. "We'll tell people you're a mail-order bride because you were. Let's grow old together, Millie. You'll be Millie Hawkins and I'll protect you until my dying day."

She started sobbing hard. The sound cut right through him quicker than the sharpest knife ever could. Because it was not the crying of a happy woman—far from it. It was the sound of a heart breaking. And the thing was, he didn't know if it was his heart or hers because the answer was *I can't*, not *I will*.

"I haven't earned my keep," she wept. "I owe Mistress too much."

Anger flared and caught within his chest. "I thought you were here by choice. I came all this way looking for a woman who hadn't been forced. Is she hurting you?"

Millie shook her head, leaving his shoulder damp with her tears. "It's not like that." She sniffed hard and leaned back, staring up into Matthew's face. Her nose was red and her eyes were bloodshot but she was still the most beautiful woman he'd ever seen. "She spent months training me, hundreds of dollars on my clothes. I haven't…" She swallowed hard a few times, tears running down her cheeks again. "I can't

63

guarantee she won't come looking for me and she's a lot sharper than George ever was. She has connections. She *knows* people."

"I can protect you." But even as he said it, he knew what she would say. Then a thought occurred to him. "Unless you're not interested." She looked horrified and he heard himself just keep going because if she didn't want him, then he needed to know why. "Is it because my daddy was black? Or my son's mother—that she was Mexican? Just tell me. I can take it."

He wasn't entirely sure how true that was because this was only the second time he'd ever fallen in love. When his Maria had died, it had damn near killed him, too. If he hadn't had to take care of Jed, he might have just given up and limped off into the sunset.

It wouldn't be that way this time, would it? It wasn't like Millie was going to die.

Would she?

Every now and then, a story would make the paper or be told around the stove at the general store in Decatur about a whore who got cut up or beat to death by some sick bastard. Just because this was supposed to be the finest brothel in the state of Texas didn't mean that Millie wouldn't run into a customer who would do her harm just because he could. Or she could get with child. Would her Mistress get her a good doctor to help with the birth? Or would Millie bleed out, just like Maria had done?

If she refused him, would he spend the rest of his days worrying over her? Would he ever be able to let go of her memory?

The next thing he knew, Millie was kissing him— hard. "How could you think it matters? Of course it doesn't, Matthew," she scolded when she pulled back, right before slanting her lips over his again. "Of course it doesn't. You're the best man I've ever met and I want to be your wife. More than anything, I want you."

He went hard as she kissed him again and again. She shifted, straddling him and his cock found her slit on its own. He slid into her body in one long thrust and they both moaned with the pleasure of it. "Say it again," he whispered into her hair.

"I want you, Matthew. Only you." She rose and fell on him in a maddening rhythm. Water sloshed over the edge of the tub and he had to brace himself with his weak leg to keep from sliding around and losing his grip on her, but he didn't care because she wanted him. Only him.

"You're mine, Millie," he growled, digging his hands into her ass and thrusting harder. It felt like the Devil himself had possessed him and he couldn't stop claiming her. "Mine and mine alone."

"Yes," she gasped, throwing her head back. "Yours."

"Again. Say it again." He managed to catch her nipple in his mouth and drew on it hard.

A shuddering cry broke from her lips. "I want— oh, Matthew! I want to be your wife." She sank her fingers into his hair and jerked his head back. "I want you."

He slammed into her. "*Mine.*" Her body tightened down on his and he'd already started to spurt his seed by the time he was able to lift her off him.

She collapsed into his arms and he held her, his heart hammering wildly. She wanted him. God, it was a good thing. "Will you come with me? Tonight?"

65

"I can't."

Some of his passion cooled. "Can't? Or won't? You know I can give you the life you want, Millie. A home, a family. A husband. *Me*."

"I don't want to be a whore anymore," she whispered, wrapping her arms back around his neck. "You were only the third man I'd ever been with and I thought I could sell my body without risking my soul but I can't. It's been a month and aside from you, every night has been like making the same mistake all over again. But I can't leave. Oh, Matthew—I don't want you to hate me, but I *can't*."

"Oh, sweetheart," he said, holding her even tighter. Her legs were around his waist and she was on his lap and despite the fact that she wouldn't run away with him, she still felt right in his arms. "I could never hate you. But there has to be a way." His mind spun around the problem. "I could kidnap you," he offered halfheartedly.

She made a sound that was half sob, half chuckle. "Let me think on it," she said, her voice soft in his ear. "I tried not to think about leaving because I didn't have any place else to go—but…"

"Your place is with me. Always." He'd burn through a lifetime supply of candles leaving a light in the window for her, if he had to.

She leaned back and gave him a watery smile. "Leave me directions how to find you. If I can figure a way, I'll come."

He stroked his thumbs over her cheek, trying to erase the tracks of her sorrow. He didn't like her answer but what was he supposed to do here? Tie her up and drag her out of here? Even if it worked, it would be taking her choice away from her—and that was why she'd run away to Texas in the first place, wasn't it? Because her rotten half-brother had decided he could do what he wanted with her.

So as much as it killed Matthew to even think of leaving her here, he knew he'd have to swallow his pride. He let a long breath out and forced himself to say, "I'll do that. Let me hold you, sweetheart. I'll wait for you, only let me hold you now."

"I'll find a way," she promised. "I'll come to you, Matthew, I swear it."

All he could do was hope that was a promise she meant to keep.

Chapter Eight

Saturday was when all the Jewels spread their money around the shops in Brimstone. They wore perfectly respectable day dresses in their colors, flirted with everyone above a certain age and never, ever haggled over price—Mistress's orders.

Millie normally went with Emerald Green and was often joined by Ebony White, but today she hung the back.

It had been three days since Matthew had left. Three days that had almost driven her to madness.

She couldn't take much more of this life. How had she ever thought she could abandon not just propriety, but her hopes and dreams? Because every gentleman caller she brought off felt like another nail in her coffin.

Surely, Mistress would release her from her obligations. Millie was not a very good whore. She tried her hardest, but this wasn't who she was. She hadn't saved up very much, but Millie had managed to put fifty dollars in the bank since she'd started. It wouldn't cover the cost of her dresses or of her meals, but Mistress had made that great speech about how, if Millie became a Jewel, it would always be her choice.

Well, Matthew was her choice.

She paused at the door to the parlor and took a deep

breath, trying to work up her nerves. She was twenty now and at no point had she magically gotten better at standing up for herself. Rather than confront George, she'd run away. Rather than demand her new husband be gentle with her, she had laid there and suffered quietly. And rather than leave before now, she had grit her teeth and tried to envision her future after she left this place.

Even now, she could see it. She wouldn't wear gowns like this, but simple dresses that allowed her to move freely. She'd bake fresh bread and wash the dishes and teach Jed his numbers and letters while they fed the chickens and weeded the gardens together. He'd be a good boy, sweet and a little naughty, and he'd look like his father.

And when Matthew came in at the end of the day, they'd share a meal together and read stories curled up in front of the fire and when Jed finally went to bed, she would massage Matthew's leg and he'd rub her shoulders and they'd keep a candle lit so they could watch *exactly* what they did to each other in the sanctity of the marriage bed. It was so real she could almost taste it, that vision. A loving husband, a family—happiness.

All she had to do to get it was walk away.

Mistress was standing by the window of the parlor, staring hard at something outside. One hand pressed against her lips and the other covered her heart. She didn't move as Millie stepped into the room, which wasn't like Mistress. She was always aware of her surroundings. It was one of the reasons Millie didn't feel like she could just slip out the back door— Mistress would know. It was like a sixth sense for her.

Her curiosity aroused, Millie took another step

closer and looked out the window. She didn't see anything unusual, just a black man standing across the street, his hands in his pockets as he stared at the brothel. But when Millie looked back at Mistress, she looked as if her heart was being torn out of her body. She looked *wounded*, for God sake.

"Mistress?"

"What?" Mistress snapped. Millie jumped in shock at Mistress's harsh tone, but then Mistress saw her and an impressive change came over her. Her shoulders relaxed and she dropped her hands to her waist and her face softened into her usual welcoming smile as she said in her usual voice, "Oh, Topaz. Was there something you needed?"

No, not her usual smile. Millie could see the strain in the corners of her mouth and around her eyes. "Are you all right, Mistress?"

The older woman made a dismissive motion with her hands. "Of course, dear. Why wouldn't I be?" But her face told a different story.

Millie took another step into the room. The black man was still standing there. "Who is he?"

Mistress's smile got so tight it almost cracked. "No one of concern." Millie must've given her a look because Mistress said in a huff, "I believe it is the man known as Free Franklin. I don't know if you've heard of him—he lives on the far outskirts of town and is reputed to shelter runways. They say he was a conductor on the Underground Railroad, but I doubt he's up to much good. The war is over, after all." Her tone was almost too casual as she swept away from the window and sat down in her chair. "Was there something you wanted?" she asked, her voice brittle.

Millie stared at the man outside the brothel for a moment longer. He helped runaways? As Millie was white, she had no need of the Underground Railroad, but...

"Mistress, I needed to speak with you about something."

Mistress looked up from where she was pouring tea into a fine china cup. Irritation scored her brows and she looked older this afternoon than Millie had ever seen her look. "Oh? You don't want another dress, do you Topaz? Really," she said, sounding most put out, "they are quite expensive and I've spent so much money on you already. It's barely been a month!"

This was not going how Millie had planned. Mistress was already irritated, which was rare enough. How was she supposed to tell Mistress she wanted to leave now? Because this was not a woman open to letting an investment walk out the door.

Millie dropped her gaze to the floor. "No, of course not. The dresses are lovely. I..." The words *I want to leave* formed on her tongue but just then, Mistress narrowed her eyes and Millie had to wonder if maybe she'd underestimated this woman. She didn't just look irritated—right now, she looked dangerous.

And she'd heard stories. Most of the girls here had been rescued from dire straits by Mistress. Ebony? She claimed that Mistress had had her abuser beaten bloody for what he'd done to her. And although she hadn't shared her story, Emerald had nodded in agreement and said she often wondered what had happened after she'd gone with Mistress...

"Well?" Mistress demanded, her voice sharp.

71

She couldn't do it. She couldn't tip her hand because if Mistress were going to go back on her promise, then Millie would never be able to escape. "I need some more of that oil."

Which was true. She had given her jar to Matthew after she had worked his muscles again. She could tell he had been doing as she'd asked, because the hole in his leg had filled in slightly and his flexibility was much greater.

"Well, that's fine." Mistress took a slow sip of her tea, staring at Millie over the rim of her teacup. "Was there something else you wanted?" Millie shook her head no. With a great exhale of breath, Mistress sat her teacup to the side and said, "You are doing quite well, dear. The first few months are the hardest—trust me, I know. I, too, went from being a bride to...this." For a moment, Millie thought she heard regret in Mistress's voice and the older woman looked out the window, a strange look of longing on her face. But before she could dare to hope that she'd misjudged Mistress, the older woman went on in a stronger voice, "But if you can hold on, you'll never be powerless again."

If she hadn't felt like crying, Millie might have laughed out loud. *That* was what she was supposed to gain from this devil's bargain—money and power. Her choices were to be her own and she would never again be at someone else's mercies.

And yet, here she stood in the parlor, unable to tell this woman who had been kind to her that she couldn't "hang on" for another few months. Topaz Gold was not who she was. And she could never be someone like Mistress.

"Thank you, Mistress." Millie ducked her head. "Is there anything you would like me to fetch you from the shops?"

Mistress's eyes grew distant she stared out the window again. "No, my dear. There's nothing out there I want."

Millie gave a little curtsy and backed out of the room, thankful to be free from Mistress's strange mood. But she was no closer to a solution to her problems. Matthew would wait for her, but how long? How much longer could he accept that she let other men fuck her instead of making her escape to him? Weeks? Months? Not years. Not as long as it would take to repay what Mistress had spent on her.

After she donned her shawl and bonnet, she stepped outside. It was dusty in Brimstone, with the unpleasant smell that came with too little rain to wash the streets clean. She headed toward the dry-goods store, clutching her reticule to her side. It took effort to hold her head up and smile as she passed by people. A few men tipped their hat—and a few ladies glared at her.

She ignored them all and tried to think. She shouldn't have tried to talk to Mistress, not when she was in a mood. Instead, Millie should have left with Emerald and Ebony. She did not want to stand out in the crowd right now. She just wanted to blend and hide, like she had her first few nights at the Jeweled Ladies. Before Matthew had come into her life.

She wanted to cry. But crying was a waste of energy and it wouldn't solve any of her problems. She couldn't slip into the shadows and disappear so she needed to figure out a solution.

Lost in thought, she rounded the corner and ran headlong into someone. "Oh!"

Strong hands steadied her by the elbow. "Miss, my deepest apologies. I did not see you there."

Millie stepped back and realized she was face-to-face with Free Franklin, the man who had been watching the brothel. "I am at fault, sir," she said, feeling worse by the second. She remembered to bat her eyes at him, but she didn't have to work up a blush. It was happening anyway. "I was lost in thought."

Franklin dropped his hand away from her elbow and took a step back. He gave her an informal bow. "You're one of Mistress's girls?"

Millie's blush deepened. "Yes." What she was supposed to do was flirt and entice and encourage this man to come by the brothel and spend his hard-earned money on her or another girl to his liking.

But that's not what she did. Instead, she lowered her voice and leaned toward him to say, "Do you really help runaways?"

Something in his eyes shuttered. "That's the rumor, all right."

That was neither a denial nor an acknowledgment. "Sir," she said, a wild and desperate hope trying to take hold of her. "I am one of Mistress's Jewels, but I've made a terrible mistake and I don't know how to get away. I don't think she's going to let me leave."

Franklin's eyebrows jumped up and he looked concerned. "Walk with me, miss…"

"Topaz. Topaz Gold."

"Miss Gold," he said, sounding genial about it as if they really were just two strangers remarking upon the fine weather. "Have you spoken with your Mistress about this? I always heard she was a mighty fair woman. Never kept anything or anyone against their wishes."

They were a block away from the dry-goods store and there, Millie knew that their paths would diverge. "I tried, but she has spent a great deal of time and money on me and I have not earned my keep. Everyone works—except..."

"It's not an easy life, I've heard."

"It's a terrible life." She couldn't keep the bitterness out of her voice but she did manage to keep from crying, so that counted for something.

They passed a few steps in silence. People paused to turn and look at them, and Millie focused on spreading her smiles everywhere except at the man walking next to her.

"You have a place to go? I understand that everyone who winds up there doesn't have anywhere else to be. That's why they stay."

"One of my...gentlemen callers—he's a rancher. He asked me to marry him and help raise his son and I would love nothing more than to be a wife and a mother. Not this." She looked down at her shimmering day dress. "I don't ever want to wear gold again."

They were almost to the store now. Other Jewels were doing their shopping there and they might note that she was talking with Free Franklin. They might carry word of this conversation back to Mistress and, given Mistress's reactions in the parlor, Millie knew that wouldn't be a good thing.

"My place is five miles west, along the edge of Sugarbush Creek. I can hide you for a few days—but I won't risk my neck over you, Miss. I'm might fond of it."

75

Millie exhaled in her relief, a wide grin she didn't have to fake breaking over her face. "I need to get north. My intended is a rancher outside Decatur. I only have fifty dollars in the bank—and I'll give most of it to you."

He stopped and took her hand, bending over it. "I don't believe the Jeweled Ladies is open on Sunday. If you can get away, they may not realize you've gone until Monday evening. But make sure you aren't followed. Then we'll see about getting you to Decatur."

"Oh, thank you, sir." Millie almost threw her arms around his neck and hugged him in gratitude, but just then, a sour looking woman in a terrible dress went past, sniffing in distaste.

Franklin tipped his hat and, without another word, spun on his heel and walked away. Millie took a second to check her reflection in a store window, trying to pull off an air of Devil-may-care attitude, as if she'd just had a successful negotiation that would bear fruit later tonight.

This was what she would do. She would go to the bank and, instead of depositing this week's wages, would withdraw her meager nest egg. She didn't know if she could get away tomorrow, but by the next week, she would be packed and ready to go. Mistress encouraged her Jewels to go to church—and then they had the rest of the day off. She would... She would claim a headache. Yes, that was what she would do. She could walk five miles in a day and if she wore an old dress of hers, people wouldn't see a runaway whore. They'd only see a woman.

She could get to Franklin's and then, somehow, she would get north to Matthew.

This had to work. It simply had to.

Chapter Nine

Please take care of Papa and me and please bring me a puppy and a mommy. Amen." Jed scrambled off his knees and under the covers.

Bless the boy, he couldn't know how the nightly prayer for a mother weighed heavy on Matthew's heart. Matthew had a puppy lined up for Christmas in two months but as for a mommy...

Matthew tucked the blankets up tight around his chin and smiled down at his son. The boy looked up at Matthew with his big brown eyes, soft and happy and hopeful that maybe God would answer his prayers. "What did you pray for, Papa?"

Matthew made himself smile as he stroked Jed's soft hair. "For a mild winter and a good calving season." And Millie. He prayed and prayed and prayed that the woman would get word to him that he should come fetch her. It didn't matter from where. He'd travel to Boston if he had to, just so long as he could bring her home and feel whole again.

His leg began to throb from kneeling. Matthew slowly got to his feet. He couldn't dwell. If she wrote, then she wrote. And if she didn't...

In another month or so, he'd be able to take another trip down to Brimstone. He'd pick up a puppy for Jed and try his damnedest to bring Millie home with him. But if she said no again, what would he do? Keep on as he had been, working his cattle in the day and doing his best to raise his son by night? Would he try to order his own bride? Or would he pick a local widow, someone who would be more of a grandmother than a mother to Jed?

He didn't want to do any of those things. He just wanted Millie.

He sat on the edge of the bed and smoothed out the boy's blankets. Mrs. MacKay had fashioned a ragdoll for the boy, although she claimed he was a soldier and not a doll. Matthew hadn't minded. Jed needed something to keep him company. He made sure Private Stuffy, as Jed had taken to calling his little soldier, was tucked in next to Jed. "You're on guard duty, Private Stuffy," he said in a serious sounding voice that made Jed giggle. "Defend the house with honor."

"Daddy, Private Stuffy's not real," Jed said, smiling big.

"Are you sure?" Matthew smiled and squinted down at the doll, as if he didn't trust what he was seeing. But he was really watching his son. He was a handsome lad, all the more so because Matthew could see Maria in him. "Tomorrow's a big day—we're headed into town. If someone can behave, they might get a peppermint stick from the general store." He gave Private Stuffy a hard look.

Jed broke out in a fresh round of giggles, all childhood innocence and joy. He tilted his head toward his doll and nodded, as if that bundle of cloth had said something. "Private Stuffy says he's going to be on his best behavior, Papa. He likes peppermint sticks a whole bunch."

Matthew nodded and pushed himself to his feet. He needed to rub the oil Mellie had given him into the scar tissue. "Goodnight, son. See you in the morning."

"Night, Papa."

Matthew blew out the candle but stood there for a moment, listening as his son settled in and began breathing deep and regular. When the boy had been born, it had been like someone had taken Matthew's heart out of his body and now it was out walking and talking and carrying on conversations with a rag doll.

Quietly, Matthew climbed down from the loft. He stripped off his britches and began digging into the scar tissue with Millie's oil. It filled the small cabin with her scent, torturing him all over again.

He was trying to do the right thing. He was giving her the space she needed to make her own decisions and solve her own problems. Besides, he was a black man. Although he got on well with his neighbors, he couldn't just go *take* Millie. The law frowned mighty hard on a black man kidnapping a white woman and, as much as he wanted her, he couldn't risk his neck. Because it wouldn't just be his neck—it would be Jed's, suddenly without a mother or a father.

Maybe he'd pay the money to send her a telegram tomorrow. It would mean letting the town know his business but he could word it so it didn't sound sinful. Yeah, he'd do that. Just to see how she was. Just to let her know that he was still here, waiting.

Because what else could he do but wait?

The trip into Decatur took the better part of the morning. If Matthew had been able to ride Smoky, his horse, he could've made it in an hour or so. But

79

hitching up the wagon and wrangling Jed was a different beast altogether. By the time they made the city limits, Jed was hungry and whining and Matthew was beginning to doubt that anyone would get peppermint sticks today. Least of all Private Stuffy and certainly not him. Because he was in a temper and he wasn't being as patient with the boy as he should be.

He tried to focus on his blessings. He had money in the bank. His credit was good with the storekeepers and they gave him goods at a fair price. His wagon was in sound repair and his cattle were healthy. Once Jed got some food into his belly, the boy would perk up again because peppermint sticks were a special treat that they all enjoyed. And then, if Matthew were a little bit lucky, Jed would doze on the long ride home.

It took a lot of effort to be this positive when all Matthew wanted to do was unhitch the horse and ride hell for leather to Brimstone.

"Afternoon, Hawkins," said Davidson, the owner the dry-goods store. He snapped his suspenders and leaned down over the counter. "And afternoon, Mr. Jed. How are you on this fine Saturday?"

"If I'm good, Papa is going to buy me and Private Stuffy peppermint sticks," Jed announced.

Davidson smiled big and a woman Matthew had seen around a few times giggled and batted her eyes at him. Mrs...Jenkins, he thought. A war widow, although she was considerably older than Matthew was, by at least ten years. The odds of getting her with child would be slim, which was a point in her favor. She wore a fine blue dress and had a pleasant-enough face but when he tipped his hat in her direction and she beamed at him, Matthew felt...

Nothing. Not a damn thing. The thought of bedding Mrs. Jenkins left his heart—and his cock—limp.

"You got a telegram," Davidson said, sounding just as surprised about this as Matthew felt.

"I did? I was thinking of sending one, but I didn't think I'd get an answer before that." He tried to smile, but his mind was spinning fast. Was there anyone who would send him a telegram besides Millie? "When did it come in?"

"Two days ago," Davidson said, digging through stacks of telegrams until he found the right one. "I thought you'd be by today, so..." He shrugged and handed it over.

"Thanks," Matthew said, his heart jumping up in his throat. It had to be from Millie. Although if it was...Davidson had probably already read it. In fact, more people in this town probably knew what his telegram said than he did. "Jed, why don't you pick out a peppermint stick?"

"Does Private Stuffy get one, too?" Jed said, turning big eyes up to Matthew and looking hopeful.

If it bought him another fifteen minutes of quiet, then... "He has to save his for after dinner." Davidson got the hint and led Jed off to the jars of candy, where serious discussion on the merits of peppermint sticks versus taffy broke out. Matthew stepped to the corner of the counter, affording him just a little more privacy from the other people milling about.

"Will be arriving Saturday, 4 PM stage stop *excited to meet you* stop *your mail order bride Mildred* stop*"*

Mildred? Either he'd lost his mind or she was covering her tracks. She'd said Millicent—but she'd also said that she was worried her vile half-brother would track her down.

Slowly, as if he were moving through molasses, he looked up at the clock on the wall. He didn't want to lose his mind. He wanted this to be real. He wanted Mildred to be Millie and he wanted her here *now*.

Four fifteen.

Matthew read the telegram again—and again, just to be extra sure. Hope built slowly in his chest and then, all of a sudden, it exploded, damn near rocking him off his feet. She was coming?

She *was* coming. Now. Right now—because there was the stage, coming to a stop in front of the hotel. She was here. God, he hoped she was here.

Matthew couldn't move. His lungs wouldn't work and his legs were of no use at all.

Matthew didn't often relive his battalion's defeat at the battle of Galveston but right now? It was as if the fight still raged on inside of his head. Because the prickling awareness that he'd had as the cannonballs had whistled overhead, the way his stomach seized up as the Rebs had surging forth, how his body tensed up seconds before the bullet had ripped through his leg.

It was the same now and yet it was different because it wasn't a sick dread that had him frozen in place, but an untamed kind of hope. He wasn't watching helplessly as his life was blown to bits and damn near ended.

He was watching his life start over again. Maybe. He hoped like hell that whatever happened, from this moment on, didn't leave him torn to shreds.

Dumbly, he looked over to Davidson, who gave him a big smile and snapped his suspenders again.

"You didn't tell me you had ordered a bride," he said, humor lacing his voice.

"It was a surprise," Matthew said. Even to his own ears, his voice sounded dumb. "Wasn't sure when she'd be coming."

"Best go meet her. I'll keep Jed here with me—he can help me inventory the peppermint sticks," Davidson said with a wink at Jed, who giggled and hopped up and down. Clearly, the boy didn't grasp the meaning of the word *bride*.

It was a kindness that Matthew would never forget because he had to make sure it was Millie, really and truly—and that she was here and his free and clear, that she still wanted to be his wife and Jed's mother. He didn't want to introduce his son to her if that wasn't going to come to pass. It would be bad enough if his heart broke. He couldn't bear to break Jed's heart, too.

He all but stumbled out of the general store and down the wooden steps. The stage was emptying itself of passengers—it looked like the whole thing was full. Bags were being thrown off the roof and people were stretching their aching backs and he didn't see her. Where was she?

The women milling around the hotel's front steps weren't dressed in glamorous gowns or shimmering gold. Although they were all respectably dressed in blues and browns and plaids, every one of them were creased and travel worn.

Then the crowd parted and there *she* was. Not Miss Topaz Gold, not Goldie—but Millie. Her traveling dress was a deep green, her bonnet a plain straw. She had a faded carpetbag in her hands and a white shawl tucked around her shoulders.

He sucked in air as if he'd been shot again, except instead of pain, there was joy. So much joy because there was his heart, walking around on the outside of his body again.

He felt it deep in his bones when she saw him. As much as he wanted to sweep her off her feet and laugh with the wonder of it all, he didn't. They had a fiction to maintain—they'd never met before. Never even clapped eyes on each other. She was a respectable young woman looking to settle down and he was a lonely rancher. That was their story and, by God, he was going to stick to it. He would never breathe a word of the Jeweled Ladies to a single soul in this town.

He made his way across the street, the slow pace pulling at his bad leg. The whole time, he stared at her in wonder. She'd come.

"Ma'am," he said, tipping his hat when he got in front of her. "Would you be Mildred?"

"I am Mildred Townsend," she said, her voice soft with a little hint of a tremor. "Are you Matthew Hawkins?"

The crowd swirled and parted around them as they played their parts, but Matthew couldn't see or hear anyone other than Millie. By God, she was the most perfect thing he'd ever seen. "I am. It was right good of you to come. I wasn't sure if you'd make it."

Her cheeks colored a soft rose. She didn't have on any makeup, he realized—she was prettier for it. "Travel plans proved more challenging than I would've liked," she admitted. "I came as soon as I could."

The effort it took to not pull her into his arms, to

not kiss her, to not even stroke his fingertips over her cheeks was painful. Oddly, though, he didn't want to touch her, not until they were married and could start anew. Not until she was his and he was hers.

"Thank you for meeting me," she said, sounding a little shy about it. "I was hoping that the offer of marriage still stood?"

He wanted to throw his hat in the air and laugh and whoop it up. But he didn't. "It surely does. But maybe you'd like to meet my son before you make your final decision?"

Her innocent demeanor cracked as she shot him a look that was half frustration, half amusement. "I don't intend to go back on my word. But if he's here…"

"Papa? Mr. Davidson said I was so good that I could have another peppermint stick," Jed said, rocketing toward Matthew at top speed, Private Stuffy trailing in his hand. He pulled up short when he saw Millie. "Who are you?"

"Jed Hawkins, is that any way to speak to a lady?"

Jed scuffed his toe in the dirt, his head low. "How do, miss," he said, sounding like Matthew was torturing him. But then the boy lifted his head and peered at Millie.

Millie took a deep breath, her hand over her heart. Then she crouched down, getting to Jed's eye level. "Hello, young man. I was thinking that maybe I could be your mother. Would you like that?"

Jed jolted as if someone had stabbed him with a pin. "But it's not even Christmas," he exclaimed, which made Matthew chuckle and drew a confused look from Millie.

"Maybe we don't have to wait for Christmas to get a mother," Matthew said, unable to take his eyes off this woman. She was really here. And Jed was right—it wasn't even Christmas. But she was trimmed in a green gown and he couldn't wait to unwrap her.

Later. Wedding first, unwrapping second. Millie straightened, smiling sweetly to the boy. "Will you be a momma to Private Stuffy, too?" he asked, holding up the rag doll. "And do you like puppies?"

"Of course," she said easily. "I'm looking forward to a whole houseful of big, strong men and a nice puppy to guard us all." As she said it, her gaze lingered on Matthew.

He had to get her out of this street before he made a fool of himself. "Shall we find the preacher?" Or the judge. Or anyone who could marry them right *now*.

She held out a hand to Jed and he took it. His hand was no doubt sticky with peppermint, but Millie didn't seemed to mind and that was when Matthew realized this was all happening. Millie was real and she'd come for him and she'd love Jed like her own flesh and blood. "Let's get married," she said, a secret smile tucked in the corner of her mouth just for him. She extended her other hand to him. "And then we can go home."

Home. There'd never been a sweeter word. He laced his fingers with hers and then, unable to stop himself, he pressed a kiss to her cheek. "Home is where you are, sweetheart."

Epilogue

One year later…

Matthew paced around the porch, trying to keep his calm even as all he wanted to do was rush into the cabin and demand that Mrs. MacKay and the doctor do something—anything.

He'd promised to protect her—but how could he when she was giving birth? He'd failed her. He shouldn't have gotten her pregnant. He, of all people, knew what the risks were. And the thought of losing Millie after only having her as his wife for a year made him want to lose his lunch in the bushes.

"Momma's gonna be okay, right?" Jed asked, pausing before he threw the stick for Spots. Private Stuffy sat on the steps, watching the boy and dog romp.

"Of course," Matthew lied. What if this baby was as big as Jed had been? What if Millie couldn't handle it? What if…

A guttural cry cut the air and everyone and thing—including the horses in the corral—paused and looked toward the house. Then, in the split second of silence that followed, another cry began to build—the small noises of a baby discovering his lungs.

Matthew all but collapsed on the step next to Private Stuffy and dropped his head in his hands. The baby—the baby was alive and crying. That was good. Great. But...

Millie?

Jed came and sat next to him, handing him the rag doll to hold. Spots nuzzled under his hand and whined softly. The Hawkins men sat in silence while Matthew prayed for his wife. *Please, please don't let her bleed out. Please don't take her from me. From us*, he amended, wrapping an arm around Jed's shoulders.

Then the door creaked open. "Oh, now," came the crackling Irish voice of Mrs. MacKay. "Don't be looking like someone died because everyone in here is very much alive and well."

Matthew sprang to his feet, launching Private Stuffy and sending Spots scurrying for the corral. "Is she okay? And the baby?"

Mrs. MacKay smiled kindly. She'd been with Maria when she'd bled to death and she understood Matthew's terror. She wiped her hands on her apron— Matthew tried not to note the reddish streaks on it— and rested a hand on his shoulder. "Your young wife did well, dearie. The doctor is just finishing up. And your daughter—"

"My daughter?" he got out, a strangled sound. A girl. Millie had had a girl.

"She's got a fine set of lungs on her," Mrs. MacKay noted, as if Matthew hadn't interrupted her.

"I got a baby sister!" Jed announced loudly and then he began to dance around the yard, Spots jumping and barking at his heels. Even Smoky in the corral whinnied in appreciation of the good news.

"Wash your hands and go inside. I'll stay out with Jed," Mrs. MacKay said, stepping around Matthew. "They're tired, dearie, but they're just fine."

Matthew did as he was instructed. The doctor was straightening his shirtsleeves and looking mighty pleased with himself, as if he'd done all the hard work. "Everything went smoothly," he said, smiling down at where Millie already had a little baby on her breast. "Everyone is healthy, Matthew. Your wife did fine— she was built to handle babies, I believe. I hope that's a comfort to you."

But Matthew barely heard him. He fell to his knees, bad leg be damned, and drank in the sight of his wife and daughter. Millie's curly hair sprung out in all directions, damp with sweat. Her eyes were shadowed and her face flushed a bright red but she was still the most beautiful woman he'd ever seen. All he could see of his daughter was the very top of her little head. The rest of her was swaddled tight in a new blanket.

And there she was, his heart on the outside of his body again.

"You're alive," he choked out. *Thank you, God*, he prayed. *Thank you for these gifts.* His eyes began to water. "I was afraid you wouldn't make it." Terrified, really. But he'd held it inside so he wouldn't worry her.

"Oh, Matthew." Millie leaned her head against the pillow and held out a hand to Matthew and he took it. "Come here and see what we made, darling."

"Beautiful." He burned the image of them into his mind because he never wanted to forget this. The baby girl's hair wasn't as dark as Jed's had been. She'd take after her mother, he realized. The thought filled him with a love so powerful his eyes began to water again.

"Matthew?"

He tore his gaze away from where his daughter was nursing. "Yes, love?"

"This is everything I ever wanted." She stroked the downy hair atop their daughter's head. "Thank you for this. Thank you for being my family."

"Oh, Millie." He levered himself up onto the bed and wrapped an arm around her shoulder. Together, they gazed at their baby. "You're everything I ever wanted, too."

About the Author

Thanks so much for reading this *Jeweled Ladies* story! Leaving an honest review or telling a friend what you thought is the best way to show the love for your friendly local author!

Who is Maggie Chase? Writer, reader, crafter—I've told a lot of different stories a lot of different ways as Sarah M. Anderson, but the Jeweled Ladies series marks my first foray into historical erotica. I passionately believe that every single person deserves their own happily-ever-after and my stories reflect that hope on the page.

Readers can find out more about Maggie any of the following ways:

Sign up for her newsletter:
http://bit.ly/maggiechasenews

Visit her website:
http://www.maggiechase.com

Check out her Tumblr:
http://themaggiechase.tumblr.com/

Follow on Twitter:
http://twitter.com/TheMaggieChase

Leave a review on Goodreads:
http://www.goodreads.com/maggie_chase

Get Amazon pre-order information:
www.amazon.com/author/maggiechase

Other Books by Maggie Chase

The Jeweled Ladies: The Mistress Series

His Topaz
Their Emerald
Her Ebony
His Sapphire
His Crown Jewel

The Jeweled Ladies: The Rogues Series

His Diamond
Their Amethyst

Now Available from Maggie Chase

The Mayor of Brimstone needs to marry his whore.
But will his assistant be able to satisfy them both?

Read on for an excerpt of
THEIR EMERALD
a Jeweled Ladies story

Emmy turned from her window just as Raymond entered the parlor, that mischievous smile on his face. Oh, good. His spirits were high and he looked whole. She should not have worried. "Raymond," she said, putting a note of severity into her voice.

Unlike Mistress's meandering path to her, Raymond did not stop to exchange pleasantries with anyone else in the parlor. He made straight for her and, grasping her offered hand in his, he bowed low over it before pressing his lips to her knuckles. "I do hope you can forgive me, Miss Green. My tardiness is nearly unforgivable. I can only pray that you will not hold it against me this evening."

When she met his gaze, she saw that his eyes were unusually bright. She supposed that, to the outside observer, they looked like they did every Tuesday. But she could tell something had happened—and it was something good. "Shall we?" Which was a slight breach of their protocol. Normally, they shared a drop of sherry before they adjourned to her room. But they had already lost a half an hour and she was in no mood to wait to find out what had him so jubilant. Right now, she needed the comfort he provided.

Raymond stood and tucked her hand into the corner of his elbow. His gaze never left hers as they strolled out of the parlor and took the wide staircase that led up to the second floor. Emmy was the center of his world right now. Her only regret about her arrangement with Raymond was that there would never be anything more than this.

They did not speak until her bedroom door was shut firmly behind them and she had shot the lock. She stepped into Raymond and began loosening his necktie. "What has happened?"

"My darling Emmy, it is the most extraordinary thing." She undid the buttons of his waistcoat and shirt and then she turned so that he could work at the buttons at the back of her gown. They did this every Tuesday, undressing each other like an old married couple until he was in nothing but his drawers and she in her shift. As he unlaced her corset, she exhaled in satisfaction. Oh, how she loved Tuesdays.

"Tell me," she insisted. "Do not leave me hanging on your every word."

He held her hand as she stepped out of her gown and then picked it up and shook it out for her, draping it over the top of her dressing screen. He was so thoughtful like that. "You won't believe it. I scarcely believe it myself."

Emmy moved to the bed and pulled down the covers. "Raymond, you are teasing me. What's happened? I was worried about you when you didn't show." She left out the part where she'd been worried Mistress was going to break her word. She didn't want to distract Raymond from his happiness.

She slid into bed and held the covers for him. He climbed in after her and tucked his arm around her shoulder. She curled into his warm, broad chest but she did not rest her head upon him. Instead, she propped herself up and stared down at him. "Out with it."

His smile—*oh*. It must be very good. He brushed a curl away from her forehead and said, "He kissed me."

Shock stilled her hand from ruffling the scattering of hair upon his chest. Those three words had just changed her world. "Hank?"

"Hank," Raymond repeated, glowing with happiness.

"But I thought you said… He wasn't… Are you *sure*?" Because she had been sure. Raymond had been sure until today, apparently.

She loved Raymond. Raymond loved her. But his heart belonged to Hank O'Shea and Hank did not love Raymond. Not like *that*.

Don't miss
THEIR EMERALD
By Maggie Chase
© 2017 by Maggie Chase
Sign up for the Newsletter
Check out www.maggiechase.com
for more great Jeweled Ladies stories!